QUEEN ANNE'S
LACE

A Novel by Dawn Gardner

Only in the darkness
can you see the stars
—*Martin Luther King Jr.*

∾

Some people say rain is peaceful; I hate rain. Right now, it's raining so hard it's like someone's throwing buckets of water on my windows. It makes me remember.

I got your letter a few weeks ago. It was a shock—I mean you were a shock. He never said anything about you. When I think about it, it makes sense that you would have been in his life at some point.

I'm surprised you want to meet me. Do you know what happened and how it happened? Probably not.

You seem nothing like him. That's a compliment, by the way. I would like to meet you too, but I think you should know what happened first. And if you change your mind, that's okay. For what it's worth, I am sorry. I know this kind of thing should be told face-to-face, but I just can't. I'll take the coward's way—write it and send it.

I wish it had all turned out differently. My friend Annie says wisdom comes with age, but even now, I'm not sure what I should've done, and I'm almost twenty.

Lacy Mitchell

1

I was thirteen. My parents had been drinking all day. This was no different from any other Saturday, except for the rain. Rainy days meant no escape, no chance to be outside, so I'd stay in my room and do research. Most of my books were from the school library; I had checked out *The Life of Insects* and *The Insect World* so often that I think the librarian bought extra copies just for me. The books didn't answer all my questions, but the pictures were great.

By seven o'clock, my parents' words would run together, and my father would become unpredictable, like walking by the yellow jackets' nest in our backyard. With the yellow jackets, I learned not to wear red and to stay out of their flight path, but with my father, I never learned how to stop his explosions.

I SPENT the afternoon across my bed, skimming pictures from a stack of books, looking for the moth I had seen the night before. It was chestnut brown, rust, and black with white Vs on each wing. Its body was covered in a rust velvet, and the wing colors bled into each other like watercolor paints. In the field guide of

North American moths and butterflies, I found a photo of the tulip-tree silkmoth. This was the same moth that had perched on the tree last night, but now it sat opened winged on the glossy page, allowing me to study its body. According to the guide, she—it was a she, because the Vs were bigger on the forewings—must have been trying to attract a mate.

At dinner, I pushed spaghetti around my plate, thinking about earthworms and how tulip-tree moths didn't eat. While my mother prodded me to eat, my father complained about the food and that Wickman Steel might be laying off welders. Sometimes the conversations at dinner would be previews of what kind of night it would be. It really wasn't the words but the flow of the conversation. That night, his complaints crashed like waves. My mother tried to talk to him, but she could only get out a few soothing words before the next wave. When he mentioned going back to being a traveling welder because of the money, my mother said nothing. It was going to be a bad night. I cleaned the kitchen and tried to be invisible.

"I've told you not to mess with my paper," he said.

"I'm sorry, Samuel." She swept the kitchen floor and turned her back to him.

"Is it too much to ask, Justine?" He got up from his chair and came into the kitchen. My mother continued to sweep. He swung her around to face him. "Is it? I put the paper right here, and now it's all over the fucking place." He yelled and pointed to a small table next to his chair.

"I was looking at—"

"I see what you were looking at." He held up the section of the paper. "Do you think I can't provide for my fucking family? You're not getting a goddamn job."

"I just want to help. The A&P is looking for someone to stock shelves."

Anger pushed out from between his teeth. "Dammit, Justine.

Why don't you tell the fucking world that your husband is nothing!"

She stepped away from him and focused on sweeping. With his hand, my father pinched her chin and forced her to look at him. He placed his other hand on the broom and tried to take it from my mother, but she held on. Alcohol made her braver.

She jerked her chin free and brought the broom handle to her chest. Without words, she caused an explosion.

From my mother's grip, he tore the handle and jabbed her in the stomach. Crouched over in pain, she was an open target for my father. He smacked her three times with the handle on her back. As my mother sank closer to the floor, my fingernails sank deeper into my palms. He always hit where the marks would be hidden by clothes. I used to cry, but my tears dried up a while ago.

He threw down the broom, and my mother moaned softly. It was over. My father could only use up so much energy in one beating. He went to the refrigerator and grabbed a beer, fell into the chair in the living room, and began the I-told-you speech.

"I told you before not to get me going." He lifted the beer to his lips and glared at my mother. It was almost the same tirade each time. He'd go on about how she deserved what she got, and how she made him do it, and then, after a while, he would say he was sorry. But he never meant it.

My mother got to her feet and slid herself into the bathroom. When she came out, it was always as if nothing had happened. The marks were hidden, but her eyes showed another piece of her was gone.

In the middle of that Saturday night, my mother crawled into bed with me. I didn't know why she came in my room until much later. I thought I was dreaming the banging against my bedroom door. I felt my mother next to me and knew what was happening. She had locked the door, and he wanted in.

Before I was completely awake, he kicked the door open and approached the bed, yelling, "You can't hide from me bitch." He ripped the covers off my bed, grabbed my mother's ankles and dragged her off.

I stood on the bed and screamed, "Let her go! Leave her alone!" My nose almost touched his and I screamed again, "You bastard!"

His right hand smacked my temple. From the force, my body was thrown into the corner of the window frame just above my bed. Blood dripped down the left side of my face. I closed my eyes, pressed my hand against the pain, and tried to stop the room from spinning. As he dragged my mother's body down the hallway, she clawed the walls and whimpered like a dog, begging, "Samuel, no ... no ..." He cursed at her all the way to the living room.

From the door of my room, I couldn't hear his words, but I saw what he was doing. My father held my mother tight; her arms and legs tried wildly to get free. She cried as her body bumped again and again against the end table. The lamp fell over because of his thrusting so hard inside her. He grunted like an animal, and she cried even louder. My stomach burned. I stopped myself from throwing up. I wanted to kill him. She pleaded for him to stop, but he didn't.

When he was spent, my mother slid out from under his limp body and headed for the bathroom. And I knew she'd wash his act away.

I crawled to my nightstand, pulled out the small flashlight—the one I kept for emergencies—and decided what I needed. The beam of light shined on my collection, a piece of brown cardboard with my insects. The date and where I found them was written under each one. It was mostly butterflies, and it wasn't something like you'd see in a museum, pieces of my insects were missing. The fact that they weren't perfect didn't matter to me, I looked at each one and saw beauty, and I remembered the moments I'd found them. I didn't want to leave them behind, but the board was too big, and their fragile bodies would've been ruined.

The light went to a small stack of books that held my other collections. My four-leaf clovers were pressed in the pages of my dictionary and smashed in between the pages of an old medical book were my flowers. Too heavy, I decided. I couldn't waste any more time, so I stuffed some clothes and my paperback field guide into a duffel bag. I reached deep between the mattress and the box spring and found the plastic bag that held my saved money and what I'd found in my mother's closet two days ago.

In the hallway, I listened for them. The house was quiet except for the sound of water in the bathroom. She could forget, but I wouldn't live another second being beaten or watching my mother lose her soul.

I slung my bag over my back and went into the living room. He was passed out, his pants still around his knees. I wanted to kick him as hard as I could—right in the face, so everyone could see the mark—but I didn't because that would make me just like him. I ran out the front door.

The rain hit my face like nails. I ran through the woods behind our house, through another subdivision, and to the bottom of an embankment that led to the highway. By the time I got halfway up the bank, my clothes were plastered on me, my hair dripped into my eyes, and my legs burned. The rain had turned the dirt to mud, and it took everything I had to reach the top.

2

I pushed wet hair out of my face and brushed the mud off my jeans. The highway was empty. I didn't know which way to go. After a while of walking, I saw a green road sign on the opposite side of the highway: Roanoke 10. Ten miles was not enough, but at least I was headed away from Roanoke, away from him. The cold rain pounded me. My heavy wool coat hung forgotten in the hall closet. Even if I needed something to keep me warm, I could never go home.

The strap on my duffel bag dug into my shoulder. I touched the outside of the pocket that held the things I had found in my mother's closet a few days ago. What it all meant I didn't know, but I hoped they were clues to a life that was nothing like mine. Who was Tommy Franco? And why hadn't my mother ever talked about him? Possibilities rolled around in my head. My body shivered, partly from the cold and partly because the things I'd found gave me hope.

I tried to stop the pinching of the strap by adjusting the bag, but it slipped off my shoulder and into a puddle. *Pick it up!* My father's angry voice yelled at me from the darkness. I straightened the bag on my back and yelled back into the night, "That will be the last time you ever hit me!" A wave of anger warmed me. I focused on the white line, walked faster, and wiped my face every four steps—it became a game.

"Where you goin', little missy?" a voice shouted.

I looked behind me and wiped my face. A man stood there. I couldn't see him clearly since the lights on his 18-wheeler lit his backside.

"Are you okay?" the man said.

"Oh, yeah. I'm fine."

"It's little late for a walk."

The man shifted his weight from side to side. Walking would only get me so far—my father might find me if I didn't get far enough away. A ride would put miles of distance between him and me.

The trucker came closer, and I looked for something that told me I could trust him. I noticed a gold wedding band on his left hand. He was married, but my father was married too—so, that didn't mean anything. Stretched across his belly was the face of Tweety Bird. My father would never wear a T-shirt like that. It was still too dark for me to see his face, but I decided this stranger couldn't do anything to me that was worse than the hell I'd left.

"Hey, do you think you could give me a ride?" I asked.

"Where you goin'?"

"Uh ... south."

"I'm goin' to Marion, that south enough for you?"

"That's perfect."

"C'mon then, let's go. It's too darn cold to be out here all night," he said.

I dragged my bag and soaked body up the steps and into his cab. The flood of warm air that hit me felt good. Peanuts were sprinkled over the seats and two greasy brown bags divided the cab seat. One bag was tightly rolled shut, and the other lay ripped open. The trucker shut his door and asked, "Want some peanuts?"

"No," I said, halfway standing and sitting.

"Just sweep 'em on the floor. I'll get 'em later."

I brushed the peanuts onto the floorboard, pulled my bag inside, and closed the door. I rubbed my hands together, trying to feel my fingers again. Loud static broken with men's voices blared out of a small black box. The trucker turned one of the dials and it quieted.

"You don't smoke, do you?" the trucker said as he placed the truck into gear.

"No."

"Good, I don't allow those things in my cab."

That's fine by me, I thought. He gave me a look that said it was my turn to speak. I just looked out the window. Worried that the rain had damaged the things I had found, I slowly unzipped the pocket of my duffel bag and felt inside. Everything was safe and dry in the plastic bag.

Now, I can't even remember what I'd been searching for in my mother's closet when I found the things. In the far corner on a shelf, shoeboxes were stacked; the largest boxes on the bottom. I'd reached for something in the back and my elbow knocked off the top boxes, causing them to fall into a pile on the closet floor. Bright red shoes with shiny black bows poked through a jumble of papers. The heels were skinny and long and the bottoms had few scratches. My mother never wore shoes like those.

I'd slid off my tennis shoes and socks and crammed my feet into the red stilts. My heels hung over the back, but all my toes were in. I'd wobbled around the bedroom pretending to be her, but when I stumbled into the dresser, the mirror reminded me I wasn't her. Her hair was long and golden; my hair was long but brown like my father's. My toes had gone numb, so I took off the shoes and placed them back in their box.

I'd gathered up the papers, mostly receipts and old bills. A yellow bit of newspaper caught my eye. The clipping was about a high school boy from Reidsville, North Carolina getting a basketball scholarship to Duke. Under the photo of the boy shooting a basketball, was the caption, "Tommy Franco scores winning basket for Reidsville." On top of the pile, where the clipping had been, there was a small folded piece of notebook paper with faded blue lines. I unfolded it; the paper was almost a perfect square. Overlapping lines of different colors weaved in and out and formed a circle in the center of the paper. In red ink under the design, the word *Love* was written and a cursive *T*.

As I refolded the clipping to put it back, I noticed, in a corner of the box, a small black-and-white photo of my mother and a young man. I peeled it away from the corner and stared at my mother's young face. The man's face was blurry—he must have moved when the camera snapped—but I could tell it was the same boy from the newspaper clipping. On the back of the photo, Mr. and Mrs. Tommy Franco was written, their names surrounded by hearts that hadn't been filled in. It was my mother's writing because I'd recognized her *a*'s; she wrote them like a typewriter, with a roof.

I'd shuffled through the rest of the papers and found an envelope with no return address, postmarked January 9, 1969. Inside was a letter, but before I had been able to pull it out, the front door slammed. I'd quickly thrown the rest of the paper back into the shoebox and restacked the boxes. I'd put the *Love* paper, newspaper clipping, photo and envelope under my shirt and headed for my room.

"Missy, wake up. I'm hungry, how 'bout you?"

"Sure," I said and looked out the window. The bottom of the sky was orange and purple. I had fallen asleep, but I was sure we had traveled hours away from my home. Trees trimmed both sides of the road and a row of pines grew in the middle of the four lanes. The parking lot, which held about fifteen trucks of similar size, seemed like it had been carved out of the forest because when I glanced down the road and back in the direction we traveled, there was nothing.

Past all the trucks, sat a low, sprawling building. *Cindy's Truck Stop* flashed in red neon with a white-and-pink coffee cup tipping over and back. I threw my bag over my shoulder and slid down onto the ground. The trucker came around the side to meet me. He took off a red baseball cap, and for the first time, I got a good look at his face. It was a round face trimmed in a white beard with bits of brown showing through. His ruddy cheeks made his blue eyes stand out, and there was a softness to his face.

"I guess formal introductions are in order," he said. "I'm Butch, what's your name?"

"Lacy," I shrugged.

"That's a fine name. Say it with pride." He smiled and the skin around his eyes puckered like prunes.

"I'm really hungry, Butch. Can we go and eat?" I said, not wanting to talk much.

"Sure."

Butch led the way. His blue jeans swished and his wallet chain clinked as he walked. Above the restaurant door, Don't Drive Hungry was painted in red on a piece of old wood. The paint had dripped in places, and the letters were blurred at the edges. I wondered how good the food could be.

When I stepped in, my eyes went right to a lady cooking, serving, and yelling all at the same time. She must be Cindy. Her hair was a blonde version of a black widow's spider web with snare lines that stuck out everywhere. Butch gave a nod to her as we walked to a table. The table was gray with black specks. I couldn't tell if the specks were food or paint. Butch plopped down in his seat and scooted his chair back to make room for his belly.

"Where's the bathroom?" I said.

"Go all the way down the front counter and take a right."

"Thanks."

The walls in the bathroom were the same dingy gray as the table. I washed my hands and looked into the mirror. My hair was frizzy from the rain. I pulled out my brush, wet it slightly and tried to tame my hair. My mother liked long hair, but I didn't. The brush scraped the cut, and my fingers tightened around the handle. I stood still and held my breath until the stinging stopped. I lifted my hair and looked at my father's damage; half of the cut was on my scalp and half was on my forehead, not deep enough for stitches, and a scab had already started to form.

I walked back to the table and the thought of my father waking up and wondering where I was made me smile. I was sure they didn't call the police. My mother told him something like, "She's just hiding." I used to hide, but then I learned. Take your punishment right when you're supposed to because he never forgot. It could be days later, and he'd come from behind me, and then, I'd get it twice as bad. Sometimes my mother tried to calm him before he hit me. But when his eyes glazed over and his forehead wrinkled, there was nothing that could be done.

When I reached the table, Butch had a cup of coffee and his menu was closed. I sat down and went straight to work looking at the breakfast choices. And the costs. I still didn't know how much money I had. I'd never stopped to count it—but I knew it couldn't be much. I wasn't a great saver.

A waitress came over to the table. I thought she could be Cindy's sister, same hair, same makeup. "What ya have, Butch? And who's your little friend here?"

"I'll have eggs, over easy, and bacon and a side of hash browns. And this here is Lacy, she's a friend of mine. I'm giving her a ride," Butch said.

"Well, Lacy, ain't that a pretty name." She tilted my chin with her index finger. "And with those big chocolate eyes ... I bet you melt all the boys' hearts. What ya have, sugar?"

"I'll have the French toast and an orange juice."

"All right, hon, it'll be out in just a flash."

Cindy's sister gave Butch a wink, and she was off.

Butch stared at me, and I knew what was coming. The questions: What was I doing on the highway in the middle of the night? Where were my parents? Was I running away? (He'd probably noticed the cut.) And his final question would be, How did that happen? All adults asked questions they really didn't want the answers to. And always after questions came lectures.

"What's your favorite baseball team?" Butch asked.

"What?" I said.

"Baseball ... ball, bat, men in uniforms running the bases. What's your favorite team?"

"I really don't watch much baseball."

"Lacy, everybody should have a favorite baseball team whether they watch or not. 'Cause in times like these, when someone asks you what's your favorite team, you'll know what to say."

"Okay, what's your favorite baseball team?" I said.

Butch smiled. "I'm so glad you asked. The Red Sox. There ain't no other choice as far as I'm concerned."

"The Red Sox. That's my favorite baseball team," I said, feeling the corners of my mouth moving up.

"You've got good taste," Butch said with a nod.

Silence.

The long pause that gets uncomfortable when two people talking run out of things to say. I just knew he was going to start the questions. He was about to ask me something, when the waitress brought our food.

BUTCH and I went out the door. Our conversation at breakfast had been about the weather, baseball, and peanuts. Thanks to Butch, I knew more about Virginia peanuts than I could've ever read from a school library book.

We reached the front of his truck and he said, "Lacy, do you have a place to stay?"

"No."

"Why don't you come and stay with my wife and me until you get things sorted out."

I thought about this man I barely knew and how he seemed safer to me than my own father. "Thanks, and thanks for paying for my breakfast. I could've paid. I have money," I said.

"That's all right. Thanks for the conversation. I don't usually have company on the road." Butch loosened his belt a notch, making room for his breakfast, and headed to his door. He turned back to me and said, "Listen, I hope you're not allergic to cats or dogs. 'Cause me and Betty, well ... we got a few pets."

"I love animals," I said, but I wondered exactly how many was a few.

3

I t was mid-afternoon when we pulled into Butch's driveway. White painted tires, buried halfway in the ground, were on either side of the driveway. I had asked my father once why people put tires in the ground like that. He'd said that his uncle did it to keep the drunks' cars from falling off the driveway. As he'd spoken, he'd drifted away to another time. "My aunt laid the painted tires flat, filled them with dirt and planted flowers in them. They also had a tractor tire tied to a thick branch. I loved going there just for that swing. I'd see how high I could fly." After he'd said that, he smiled. That was the only time I could remember him smiling at me. And it really hadn't been at me, it had been at his memory.

The gravel crunched under the wheels of the truck. Dead vines rested on top of a metal fence that surrounded the yard. When Butch turned off the engine, I heard a pack of dogs howling like they were dying. The front door opened and out scrambled a blur of fur. Before Butch's feet hit the ground, he was surrounded by dogs. I counted six, but I wasn't sure if the back end of one was the front end of another. "How are you doing?" he said to the pack, and they wagged their tails so hard that their backsides shook.

Butch looked toward the door, and my eyes followed his. Out came a black woman with the darkest skin I had ever seen.

"Lacy, this is my beautiful wife, Betty." Butch walked over and slid his arm into the space between her bottom and upper back, there was just enough room. They were perfect for each other; her bottom was as big as his belly. If they were two puzzle pieces, they would snap right together, except the colors would be off. He gave her a quick kiss on the cheek and slipped the rolled-up greasy paper bag into her hand. She shook it and smiled.

"Lacy, it's nice to meet you. I'm glad you didn't forget my peanuts!" Betty gave Butch a wink and said to me, "Do you like peanuts? These are the best in Virginia!"

Before I could answer her, Butch spoke. "Betty, I told Lacy she could stay with us until she gets a place of her own." He nodded his head and stared into Betty's eyes; it was as if they were speaking without saying anything.

"Well, it's a good thing I made extra cornbread for supper," Betty said and smiled.

I glided my hand over a golden dog that sat at my feet and said, "Thanks. I just need a couple of days to think and make some plans."

"Now that that's settled, how 'bout I introduce you to the family," Butch said.

"Okay," I said, watching the door for more people to come out.

Butch went down on one knee, and the dogs drooled and pranced around him. He grabbed the golden dog that had come over to me. "This here is Sparkle, and that one over there that looks just like her is Star. Star is the momma. We found them down by the railroad tracks when Sparkle was just a pup." Butch's hand reached for a tall, thin black and white dog. "This is Spot. He's a dalmatian. My neighbor's son wanted him as a pet, but he bit the boy. I might have bit that boy too. He's mean to animals." Butch stroked Spot's head. "They were gonna put him down. I said we'd take him. Come to find out, the dog can't hear a thing. So, don't sneak up behind him."

Butch struggled to get up from his bent knee. "It's hard getting old," he said as he walked over to a black dog that had plopped down after getting a pet from Butch. "This is Ray. He's our first dog. This boy is about fifteen years old. He can't see too well 'cause of the cataracts. Me and Betty sometimes call him Ray Charles."

"My goodness, Butch, get on with it. The chili and cornbread are gonna be stone cold, before you get done. And I never call Ray, Ray Charles," Betty said with her hands on her hips. She turned and went into the house.

"Monday, come here boy. Monday," Butch called. He walked around to the side of the house and I followed. A German shepherd with tall black ears came running around the corner. He sat down right at Butch's feet, his tail moved back and forth like a dust broom. "This is Monday. Guess why we call him Monday?" Butch said and smiled at me. I shrugged.

"'Cause we found him on a Monday," Butch said.

He turned toward a white tin shed. "Go on in the house and wash up. I'm gonna feed the dogs, and then we'll eat."

"COME ON BACK, honey. I'm in the kitchen," called Betty. The kitchen was small with brown paneled walls and light-blue curtains with a frilly lace and tiny white polka dots. Betty pointed to the chair at the round table and I sat. On the wall above the table was a collection of salt and pepper shakers from different places. My arm stuck to something on the green plastic mat; it looked like dried grape jelly.

"Oh Lordy, that's hot!" Betty said as her fingers danced on the handle of the pot lid. She stirred her chili and hummed. She was almost as wide as the stove. My mother was so small—it would have taken three of her to make one Betty—and she never hummed or seemed happy when she cooked.

Something rubbed against my leg. I looked down and ran my hand over the back of a light-orange cat. Its motor started and the next thing I knew, the cat had perched itself in my lap.

"Oh, if she's bothering you, just put her down."

"No, she's no bother. She's really sweet. What's her name?"

"That's Hoppy. We call her that 'cause she's only got three feet. When she walks, she hops along. Butch found her a few winters ago in the Piggly Wiggly parking lot. Poor thing, we think someone ran over her." Betty fished the butter out of the refrigerator, scooped up the cornbread with her free hand and brought both to the table. Hoppy purred louder and nudged my hand for more rubbing.

"Butch took her to the vet. We didn't think she'd make it. One of her lungs collapsed from the weight of the car. And by the grace of God, she lived. Now, she's only got one lung. But don't you know, her left lung grew longer to make up for the crushed one. Amazing, huh?" My hand smoothed over Hoppy's back, and her tail shot into the air and danced like a charmed snake. Betty laughed. "She loves attention like that."

Betty's face crinkled as she laughed, and I thought of my friend Jon—his skin was almost as dark as Betty's. When I would tell him a good joke, he would laugh. I think Jon had the prettiest teeth I'd ever seen. Jon and his family lived one street over and we usually spent our time together at his house, except if we were sure my father wasn't home. My father hated Jon, but he didn't even know him.

The last time I'd seen Jon, was on a hot August day, and we'd both been twelve. I had just turned twelve, and Jon was about to be thirteen in a few days. He always teased me about being older. We decided to escape the sun and went under the maple in the far back part of my yard. The branches were low; it had been the perfect place to keep cool. We'd laid down on our backs—this was how we'd done our best talking. It seemed words had come easier when we didn't have to look at each other. We'd called those our tree talks even though we'd mostly just stare through the leaves at the bits of sky. Sometimes, Jon would tell me about his basketball team, or we'd tell each other our favorite songs. Jon was a great listener. I'd liked him a lot, but I knew I shouldn't have liked him at all.

Hair had stuck to the back of my neck, and a long strand of my ponytail wrapped across my neck. Sweat beads had rolled down my face, tickling inside my ears. A light breeze came and I closed my eyes. Jon leaned over me, and his lips were on top of mine.

"Get your ass outta here," my father screamed. He'd come home early, taken out the trash, and saw everything. Thundering across the yard, he'd screamed, "I'm gonna kill you."

Jon scrambled to get to his feet. My father's long arms and hands reached out for him. Jon grabbed at the dirt, pulling himself up on his feet, but not before the angry hands reached the bottom of his shirt. "Don't ever touch her again, you hear me," my father shouted. Jon dropped to the ground and started rolling. Somehow, he'd wiggled free. My father chased Jon all the way to his house. I could hear him yelling in front of Jon's house. "Keep your boy away from my daughter, or I'll kill his ass!"

I'd rolled onto my back and was still. All the neighbors knew my father, I mean really knew him. They even knew about Saturdays. When I think back, I know that all the neighbors felt sorry for my mother and me. They hadn't felt sorry enough to do anything about it though. One thing they knew ... if my father said he would kill someone, he probably meant it.

I'd heard his breathing as he approached the tree, and my body trembled. His hands shot into the quiet place under the tree, I was still. "Get out here, you little whore," my father said as his hands reached my hair. He jerked, ramming my cheek against the trunk of the tree. He pulled harder and stood over me, his hands tangled with my hair, "What have you got to say for yourself?"

I knew what was ahead. It was always better not to answer any questions. I could stop my mouth, but not my eyes. Tears rolled down my face. "Those tears ain't gonna help you. Stop it, stop it!" he shouted. He lifted my head and his open hand swept across my face. I went silent. With one hand, he'd loosened his belt, and with the other, he'd dragged me by the hair to the house like a bag of trash.

"That chili smells good!" Butch yelled as he came in the front door.

At the sound of Butch's voice, I became aware that Betty was staring at me. I wondered if she had asked me a question—if she had, I hadn't heard anything. Butch came into the kitchen and touched my shoulder and said, "Why don't you go and wash up before dinner."

MY STAY with Butch and Betty turned quickly into a couple of weeks. I learned Betty's secret ingredient for her cornbread: coconut milk. She made me swear to take it to my grave. Betty talked constantly, I heard about her family reunions, growing up with five brothers, her parents, birthday parties spent in the park, and her many nieces and nephews. She had so much family, I couldn't remember any of their names. I asked Betty once why she and Butch didn't have any kids of their own. She mumbled something about her plumbing not being right and how the animals were enough to take care of.

I wondered what it would have been like to have brothers or sisters. Or even cousins. Both of my parents were only children, like me. So, when my grandfather died seven years ago, it was just the three of us. Even before he died, our family wasn't like Betty's. My grandfather hadn't come over for dinners, I'd never gone to a family reunion, and we didn't celebrate birthdays in the park.

He'd owned a store downtown, and my father and I would visit it once in a while. The store had everything—food, tools, some clothing, and a couple of pinball machines in the corner. Dirty magazines lined the space underneath the cash register. While my father and grandfather had talked in between customers, I'd pretended not to look at the magazines. Their conversations were always short, and the words between them were forced, like the trickle water from a pinched hose.

A glass jar of fireball jawbreakers had sat next to the register. My grandfather must have thought my long glances were at the red jawbreakers because every time we would leave, he pitched me one and said, "Don't let it burn a hole in your gum." He'd been the only grandparent or extended family I'd known.

My mother's parents had died when she was eighteen. Both my middle name, Marie, and Italian nose came from my mother's mother. I liked Marie, but my nose, I'd always thought was too long. When I was younger, my mother had told me stories about her parents, mostly about her mother's cooking. My mother tried over and over again to make her mother's gnocchi, but there was always something not right, and they never tasted like the ones she remembered. Once, when we were alone for a weekend, she told me how her parents died. It was a car accident; her father had fallen asleep at the wheel. She'd cried and said she'd never felt so alone and lost. It hadn't mattered to me that she was drunk—I remembered feeling like an adult because she had shared something real with me.

It was funny, I was alone, but I didn't feel lost. I wanted answers, and I wanted my life to be something other than what it had been. I pulled the letter from my duffel bag and read it again.

DEAR JUSTINE,

I'm sorry for just showing up. I was sure if I called to ask if I could come by, you would have said no. I didn't want to cause trouble for you and I didn't want to upset you. I screwed things up between us before. I was trying to make it right.

Ever since graduation, I've thought about when you came to see me on that New Year's Eve. You looked so good. Now, I can't even remember the name of the girl I was with that night. I deserved every name you called me. You were so angry, that's why I didn't believe you. But after seeing Lacy, I don't believe what you told me a few weeks ago in your living room. Did you say it for Samuel's sake? I was right to tell him that she was mine. Maybe I was an asshole, but you're lying to one of us.

Justine, you were the best thing in my life, and I was just too stupid to realize it at the time. You don't owe me anything, but I do want the truth about Lacy. I will be staying with my parents while I put out my resume. If you want to reach me, you know the address.

Tommy

FOR THE NEXT HOUR, I thought about Tommy Franco, and a memory from when I was around four years old flashed in my mind in pieces, like a collection of photos. A dark-haired man sitting in our living room talking to my mother—my mother laughing—the man reaching over and brushing a piece of hair from her face—the man smiling at me and helping me with some toy blocks—a loud crash—the coffee table cracked and the legs sticking out from underneath the wooden table top—my father and the man rolling around the living room—my mother crying on the floor.

The memory finally made sense. Tommy Franco must have been the dark-haired man, and he'd come for me. It had to be.

4

Betty and I snapped green beans for dinner, and she asked me about my family and why I'd run away. What could I say? How could she understand what happened in my family? So, I said nothing, but my thoughts went back to the night I'd left. The sound of my mother's crying and the sight of my father's face stung my mind. Betty searched my face, and I tried not to let my expression answer her question, but it didn't work because a few days later, Butch was brimming with advice.

It was a warm afternoon, and I sat in the backyard surrounded by dogs. My arm rested on Sparkle's back, and the others surrounded me, each waiting for my free hand to make its rounds. The sun warmed my nose, and the dead grass had turned green in spots. I looked down at a small hole in the ground right beside me. I ran my finger along its rim and wondered if it was an entrance to a yellow jacket nest. It was too cold now for the wasps, but in no time, the workers and guards would be buzzing around the hole and possibly a colony would be building under the ground. I wasn't afraid of yellow jackets, but I respected them. They pollinated just like honeybees;

yellow jackets, though, had more style with their tiny waists, brightly colored abdomens, and smooth stingers. And yellow jackets could sting over and over. In my backyard, I'd watch them go into the nest and come out their secret back door, which was close to the trash cans. I'd tracked their flight patterns and knew it was safest to take the trash out after dusk, when they'd all be in for the night.

At the end of that summer, my father had stood in the backyard with a can of soda and a couple yellow jackets tried to share with him. He'd swatted them away, but that was the worst thing he could've done. They attacked, and he'd jumped around, striking at the air, attracting more wasps. He'd ended up with five stings—he was lucky it hadn't been more.

The next day, he found their entrance and their secret door. I'd tried to tell him the good things about yellow jackets and how they'd die anyway when it got cold. But they had stung him, and once he'd been hurt, that was it, he wouldn't listen. He'd been determined to kill them all. At dusk, he stuffed a gasoline-soaked rag in the backdoor of their nest, buried it with some dirt, and then poured gas down their entrance before pushing a burning stick into their tunnel and setting the nest on fire. I had watched from my window as smoke seeped out of the ground.

"Spring is just around the corner," Butch said as he came up behind me. I jumped at his voice. All the dogs' tails began to wag, but they didn't move. Not one of them wanted to miss a rubbing from me. I smiled.

"I think they really like you, Lacy," Butch said. I nodded and continued to move my hand around the circle. "Spring's like magic. One day everything's brown and dead, and a day later, green covers everything and life's creeping in," Butch said as his bottom hit the ground. "Thinking about your plans?"

"Yeah," I said.

"This is a good thinking spot, ain't it?" Butch said as his hands ran over Ray's black fur. "Did you come up with anything? Can I tell you something very important?" He looked at me and I nodded. "You can run away, but holding onto the bad stuff just eats you up inside. And it don't leave just 'cause you run away." Ray pawed Butch's hand for another rub.

Keeping my eyes down on the dogs, I said, "I had to run away because of the bad stuff." There was a long pause before he spoke again.

"All I'm saying, Lacy, is that running doesn't fix nothing, and we all need people around us to lean on. Like Betty and me, you see how she takes care of me, and I take care of her." Butch stared out past the yard.

"Some families hurt. And you can't count on people to always take care of you." I hitched my chin into the air and looked in the same direction as Butch. "I don't need anybody," I said.

Butch nodded, picked up a twig and started to peel the bark with his fingernail. "I know what it's like to be loved by some-body who hurts you. My momma loved me, but she was mixed up. From how she grew up, she didn't know how to love us the right way. People ain't perfect," he said and tossed the naked twig. "My brother never forgave her." He continued, "He calls me *simple*. My brother told me once that I was too stupid to do anything but drive a truck. But I didn't pay it too much mind, 'cause he'd been drinking beer all day. I like driving a truck. I'd feel cooped up if I had to stay in one place all day. I might not be smart enough to be a bigwig like him, but I like my life."

"Do you ever see your brother?"

"Nope. But that's his doing, not mine. He's let what Mama did well up inside him. Married three times. It's been about ten years since I saw him. Last time he was here—when he was divorcing his third wife—he got drunk and threw some things around. He had done things like that before. Betty had warned me not to give him another chance. But, that's not right. I think everybody deserves chances."

"I'm sorry your brother did that," I said.

"Betty was so angry for days after he left. But I wasn't sorry that I tried to help him. The bad stuff makes me thankful. Now, I have so much good in my life. A wife who loves me and makes the best chili, my dogs, this house, my truck. I have all good stuff right now. I have a good life."

My eyes lost their focus. I thought about Tommy Franco. My life was a mistake. I was supposed to live another life—a good one. I bet Tommy gave his kids piggyback rides and held his daughter in his lap when she scraped her knee. And I bet he never hit his daughter. Why couldn't he have been my father?

He was, I decided. It made sense to me and the timing was right and he'd come back for me—why else would my mother have kept those things? And hadn't he said in the letter, *I was right to tell him she was mine*?

Butch placed his hand on my shoulder. "Lacy, sometimes the good parts are harder to see in people. Maybe someday you'll see good in your family too. Don't be like my brother."

"You don't know how it feels to have a family like mine," I said bringing my knees into my chest. My arms wrapped around my knees, and my hair draped over me, making a tent. There was no way my father was good. He hated my mother, and he hated me more. Because of some terrible mistake, I ended up with Samuel Mitchell as a father. Why had she married him and not Tommy Franco? My fingers found a strand of hair. I started to twist.

Butch reached out for Ray and scratched him behind his ears. "I think these dogs do a better job of loving than we do. What'd you think, am I right?"

I didn't say anything. I remembered my mother pushing me in a park swing when I was little. Her warm hands pressed against my back and even though I couldn't see her face, I could feel her smiling. But that was before the bottles, and in the last few years, she drank more. It seemed like she had given up—on everything. These dogs had given me more love than I had felt in a long time. Butch was probably right.

"Being alone is hard. I tell you this, and you might not believe me, but a family that ain't perfect is better than being alone in the world."

I stood up. I wasn't afraid to be alone. Butch would never understand my family and why I couldn't go back. And how could I explain that, somehow, I was someone else's daughter? How could I explain that my life had been a lie? It just didn't make sense to talk about it anymore. Butch wanted me to find some good in Samuel Mitchell, but the more I thought about it, I decided I was nothing like Samuel Mitchell. I must be Tommy Franco's daughter. And no one told me. And no one let me live the life I was supposed to.

My finger was tangled in my hair. I wiggled it free and looked at the knot I'd created at the end of my hair. I held the hair strands above the knot, grabbed the tangled hair and pulled hard. "I'm gonna see if Betty needs any help with supper," I said. I put the hair knot in my pocket and walked away, leaving Butch surrounded by his dogs.

BUTCH AND BETTY had gone to bed early and were talking softly in their room. I sat on the couch and unwrapped the paper towel packet that held the tail of a lizard the dogs had trapped that day. The lizard got away and left its wiggling tail for a decoy. The blue stripes were glittery, like the shine on an insect's wings. I wondered how animals could make parts of themselves shine like that. From their room, I heard my name a couple of times, so I crept to the end of the hallway to their door, laid on my stomach, and put my ear to the crack where the door stopped and the carpet began.

"Butch, she can't keep staying here. I don't know what we should do. She's got a family, but something bad happened. And she won't talk about it."

"Yeah, I know she's got a family, and I just know they're worried 'bout her."

"I wouldn't mind if she stayed here, but she's not like a stray animal. What if she needs special help or some kind of counseling? You and I know what animals need, but young runaway girls ... well, that's gonna be more than food and love."

Butch sighed. "I know she can't stay, but I'd hate to see her end up on the street or get hurt."

Betty's voice became soft as she spoke. "I know you want to help her, honey, but Lacy is running from something, and I don't think she wants to go back. Tomorrow, I'll call someone down at social services, they'll help Lacy better than we can."

I went to the couch and covered up. I couldn't go back, and social services would make me go home. I threw the blankets off me.

After all my stuff was in my duffel bag, I counted my money. Five dollars and thirty-four cents. I looked over at the large glass jar that Butch put his loose change in. I don't like to steal. In fact, I had only done it one other time. And that was on a dare.

My friend Jon had needed batteries for his tape player, so he'd dared me to steal some. I don't know why I'd done it. It had been stupid, and I'd known it was wrong, but when he kept teasing me about being scared, something had come over me.

When the store manager called my home, I'd been so thankful that my mother answered the phone. I'd begged her not to tell my father, and I swore I'd never steal anything again.

In the driveway, she'd grabbed my chin with her hand and stared into my face and said, "Don't you ever do that again! If your father ever found—"

My father stepped out on the front porch with his *where have you been* look, and she'd stopped in the middle of her sentence. I'll never forget the look in her eyes. I didn't hear what she'd said to him because I ran into the backyard. My mother had never said another word about it. And I knew my father never found out because—well, I'd have known if he did.

I looked at Butch's change jar again, five dollars wasn't enough. So, I took all the ones and quarters out of the jar. Twenty-one dollars and thirty-four cents. From the kitchen trash, I took a piece of junk mail with their address on it and put it in my pocket. I planned on paying them back as soon as I could. On the back of an envelope from the trash, I wrote a note to Butch and Betty thanking them for everything and apologizing for stealing sixteen dollars.

Before I left, I went to the bathroom one last time. I stood in front of the small mirror putting my hair into a ponytail. My fingers came to the spot where I'd pulled the knot from my hair. The strands were much shorter than the rest. My mother used to get after me all the time for twisting my hair, and she got mad if I broke it instead of working the hair free.

One night, as my mother had scolded me about the tangles and brushed my hair, pulling my head back with each stroke, my father came into the bathroom. He'd grabbed the brush; my mother's hands and my hair were tangled around his hand. With a quick jerk, he'd controlled the brush, popping the top of my thigh with its flat side over and over. "Next time, I'll brush your hair. And after that, you won't make any more tangles," he had said and threw the brush into the sink as he left.

I undid my hair and stared at the dark waves. I decided it was time for my hair to be the way I wanted it. Quietly, I searched the drawers, and in the bottom left-hand side, I found a pair of scissors. I placed the blades close against my scalp and cut. My hair fell. Each time hair touched my leg, I kicked the clumps away. I stepped out of the circle of hair, grabbed my bag, and opened the front door to the outside.

~

It's dark tonight; there's no moon. Living on a farm is nothing like living in the city. All the lights make it hard to see the stars. I think stars are hope. Kind of a silly thought for someone who's majoring in biology. But when I was thirteen, stars weren't balls of hydrogen and helium, they were dreams. Don't you think it's funny—the ideas we have as kids never really leave us.

This is taking me longer than I thought. I hope you received the pages I sent a few weeks ago. I've been wondering how I made it. Sometimes I doubt I will ever have the courage again that I had that year. "Comfort makes cowards," my friend Annie says.

Lacy

5

I walked a long time on the highway before anyone stopped. The trucker who picked me up told me I'd have a hard time finding anyone going to Reidsville on this part of Highway 81. "We'll head north a little ways, then you can catch a ride with a buddy of mine, straight down 77—it's not Reidsville, but it's the best I can do."

I was so happy to be riding instead of walking that I didn't care. Anywhere in North Carolina would do. I was closer to Reidsville. And that meant I was closer to Tommy Franco and farther away from Samuel Mitchell. When we reached the truck stop, I got some food and waited. Before he continued on north, the trucker radioed his friend, told him about me, and gave me a description of what his friend's truck looked like. By lunchtime, I was on my way again, in the right direction.

As we reached the trucker's destination, the sun was setting, and strips of light were shining on the gray buildings. The trucker pulled into the back of a warehouse.

"What city is this?" I asked. I had fallen asleep even though I'd tried to stay awake to watch the road signs.

"Charlotte." He handed a clipboard to the warehouse worker.

"How far is Reidsville?"

"Reidsville? That's three hours northeast of here. John didn't tell me you was trying to get to Reidsville, I would've dropped you in Winston-Salem." The trucker stretched his back and his shirt came out of his jeans, showing his thin middle. He was nothing like Butch and something I couldn't pinpoint made me not trust him. The warehouse worker flipped through his clipboard and yelled for someone in the warehouse.

After tucking in his shirt, the trucker said, "From here, I'm going south again."

Aggravated with the late shipment, the warehouse worker and the supervisor scanned the trucker's clipboard and started complaining. The three men huddled around the clipboard, their voices growing louder. I decided to find my own way to Reidsville.

I NEVER THOUGHT people could really be invisible. I had always tried at home, and it never worked. Even with hair like the spikes of a porcupine, nobody noticed me. It seemed like I had found a place where I could be invisible. Everything was crammed together—the buildings, the people. Some of the buildings were so high I had to lean my head back to see their tops. The people hurried on the sidewalks like ants, carpenter ants that followed the scent trail left by the other workers.

My stomach rumbled. I hadn't eaten in days. I moved in the ant-people line and thought about the Amazon army ants marching through the jungle and how they could make skeletons out of small mammals in minutes.

With the sunlight disappearing, we moved faster. I jumped out of the line and crossed the ant-people going the opposite direction. My stomach led me through the small alley right to the back of Naples Italian Restaurant.

I walked toward the smell. On either side of the door, trash cans exploded with noodle boxes, tomato sauce cans, and empty flour bags. On the ground was a huge yellow can with dancing black olives complete with top hats and canes. I never knew people could eat that many olives. I stood there, thinking about dancing olives and staring at the green door with *Naples* stenciled in black on it.

The door flung open, just missing my nose. I didn't even move. A hairy man with one bushy black eyebrow asked me, "Where's Flo? Are you her friend?" I couldn't speak. I'm not sure if it was because he was ten feet tall or that the tomato sauce stains on his white apron looked like blood.

"For Christ's sake, here. I gotta get back." I looked at his outstretched arm covered in black fuzzy hair. I followed his arm to his hand, and I saw a circle tin filled with spaghetti and meatballs. I couldn't speak, but I managed to take the tin. When I looked up to thank him, the green door was closed. I grabbed a meatball and crammed it into my mouth. It melted.

"Hey, you little brat!" a scratchy voice came from behind me. A skinny woman in green army pants walked to me. She grabbed the tin and said, "I'm Flo, and this is mine. Scat!" She guarded the tin and sat down against the wall of the building behind Naples. I moved closer and watched her suck the noodles through holes where she should have had teeth. As she ate, I counted four teeth on the top and three on the bottom.

"Scat, I said. Get! This is my area. Go find somewhere else," she said as a noodle slid up her chin leaving the spaghetti sauce behind. The sauce matched the color of her hair. A black knit hat pulled down on her head made two puffs of red hair stick out on either side. And her nose was big, not Italian big, but it was shaped like a ball on the end. She reminded me of Bozo the Clown. She sucked and I stared.

Flo placed the almost empty tin on the ground beside her, stood up, and came over to my face. Our noses almost touched. Her whole face was the same red as her nose, just not as dark. Flo's sky-colored eyes raked over me. "Don't you understand English? I said get!" she slurred, noodles oozing out of her mouth.

I didn't back away, but I should have; her breath made me gag. She rolled her eyes back in her head, shook her hands wild-like above her head and screamed like she was calling pigs. She looked so funny, I started to laugh. I thought of Bozo, and then I laughed louder.

She stomped back over to her spot and finished sucking her noodles. After a few minutes, she said, "Something's wrong with you. Don't you know when you're not wanted? Get on out of here!"

The green door swung open again. I turned around. The gorilla in the apron stepped into the alley using his back foot to hold the door. "Flo, next time let me know you're having guests for dinner." He handed me another tin full of spaghetti and meatballs.

"Thank you," I said. I know he heard me because I saw him smile as he went back in the restaurant. The door closed. I walked over to Flo and dropped one of my meatballs into her empty tin and said, "I'm not a brat." A few feet away, I slid down the wall of Naples and began to eat. I looked up every so often to see if Bozo was still watching me.

And she was.

FOR THE NEXT FEW WEEKS, I wandered around the city. During

the day, I found shaded places and read my field guide or magazines people had thrown away. I learned the hard way to check the dumpsters for maggots before climbing in. Usually when there were maggots, there was a smell. I didn't think it was the maggots that smelled—it was the liquids that had pooled in the bottom of the dumpsters.

I really didn't see any beauty in flies—their young were just plain-white pieces of rice that wiggle, and the adults vomit on their food before they eat it. Not my favorite insect, and I wasn't alone in my opinion. Most people hate flies and roaches, but I felt differently about roaches. They've existed for millions of years, they're one of the fastest insects, they can hold their breath underwater for forty minutes, they glue their eggs cases in concealed places, and they could possibly live nine days without their heads.

At night, I slept in the alleys and my only meal for the day was at Naples. Each night around seven, I returned to the alley and the gorilla-man gave me food. Of course, Flo got her food too. One of those nights, I heard someone call for the hairy man. They said, "Hey, Tony, it's not break time. We got customers, get your ass in here." *Tony*. I don't know what kind of name I expected, but Tony seemed to be too human. Each time he handed me the tins of food, he smiled. Unlike Flo, Tony had all his teeth. Except for the gap in between his two front teeth, his teeth were perfect and straight. He looked scary, but when he smiled, I could tell he was kind.

Tonight was a special treat. We got garlic bread with our spaghetti. The butter tasted so sweet.

"Hey, kid," Flo said interrupting my garlic bread feast.

So far, each night I'd managed to say nothing to Flo. I guessed she had hoped I wouldn't come back. I looked over at her. Her eyes wobbled. I knew that look, she was drunk. I pushed the rest of my bread into my mouth and walked over to her.

"Yeah," I said not caring about the half-chewed bread being seen.

"Where you sleeping tonight? It's gonna be cold."

"I don't know. Why do you want to know?" I questioned.

"Some nights it's cold. I don't like you, but you got spunk." Flo mumbled something as if she was talking to someone. "I am gonna tell her, just hold on," she said to the air. Looking back to me she said, "Just call this some friendly advice. Okay?"

"Okay," I said.

Flo grabbed a green bottle around its neck and took a big swig. She burped and then continued, "Don't go to the shelters. Girls are a favorite at those places. Know what I mean?" She could tell from my expression I didn't understand.

Frustrated, she spit wine and words into my face. "The men will hurt you. And if that don't happen, the people working there will send you back to where you come from. Get it now?"

"Yeah, I got it. Thanks for the tip." I walked back to finish my tin of spaghetti. She called me again.

"I wanna show you something. Come real close," Flo said as she undid the top button on her pants. I stood still for a moment. I was sure I didn't want to see whatever it was. I stepped beside her outstretched legs, leaned over to get closer, and kept myself ready to run.

"Look here." She folded down the top of her army pants. Pantyhose. Not one pair, but lots. "I got seven pairs. Seven is my lucky number," she said as she snapped each pair. Underneath the waistband of the last pair, a red blistered rash formed a ring around her stomach.

"Is it hot?" I said, trying to figure out why she wore seven pairs of pantyhose at one time. I really didn't want to ask why.

"No. And if you're smart, you'll get you some too," she said, closed her eyes and leaned back against the wall.

I walked away and picked up the tin, finishing the last of my spaghetti. It was getting dark and cold, and I needed to find a place to sleep. When she called out, I was almost out of the alley. "Tonight, take you some cardboard boxes for a bed. Go down Fifth Street all the way to the old stadium. Some of us sleep there when it's cold. Go under the bleachers, and sleep on one box and cover yourself with the other."

WHEN I REACHED THE STADIUM, I was glad to have a blanket, even if it was a cardboard one. I decided to sleep on the visitor's side. I tore each box open so they were flat. As I worked, my breath made its own fog. This was nothing like my room at home. But I didn't have to worry about him. I placed one piece of cardboard down, used my duffel bag as a pillow, and covered myself with the other piece.

Flo was right, under the bleachers was warmer than just being out in the open. From underneath, the rusted bleachers looked like a rose bush that had been eaten by a swarm of Japanese beetles. My friends at school had told me about their family camping trips; this had to be just like camping. Sleeping in an old stadium, under bleachers that would crumble if anybody stepped on them, and cardboard blankets had to top any of their pansy camping stories.

The garlic bread made my tongue pasty. Italian food had been my favorite back home. It was rare that we even went out to a restaurant since my father hated spending money on food that my mother could make. But after weeks of Italian food, I wished for a bowl of cereal. Sometimes Tony would bring us soups, sandwiches, or salads. But it was all still Italian. Flo always complained about the salads.

Samuel Mitchell had no idea how strong I was. I raised my head slightly and unzipped the side pocket of my duffel bag. My fingers touched the clipping, and I reviewed Tommy Franco's photo in my mind. His hair was curly. Yeah, it was definitely dark and curly in the photo. Samuel's hair was straight and brown. And my hair—brown and curly. More proof. I needed a plan to get to Reidsville. Tomorrow, I decided to talk with Tony. He'd help me.

WEDNESDAYS WERE ITALIAN HOAGIE NIGHT, and it was a two-for-one deal. Tony came out with our sandwiches and a special treat, a bag of potato chips for Flo and me. Sometimes, if Naples wasn't busy, Tony would sit with us, he'd smoke and talk about the weather or his five boys and his wife. "Not too busy tonight, ladies," he said as he sat down on a wooden crate.

"Thanks for the chips," I said.

"Hey, what about barbecue next time." Flo crammed her sandwich in her mouth.

"You know, Flo, beggars can't be choosers. But I'll see what I can do."

Flo stuck out her tongue and whispered to the air beside her. Tony shook out a cigarette from his pack. He thumped the skinny white stick on each end before placing it on his lips. From his pocket, he pulled out a silver lighter and with a flick of his wrist, the lighter flipped open. His lips pressed around the cigarette and his cheeks caved in. A cloud of smoke came out of his nostrils and his mouth at the same time.

"Hey, Tony, I gotta go. Do you think Lou will let me in?" Flo said, holding herself in the front and crossing her legs.

"Be quiet and Lou won't know. I mean it, Flo. Be on your best behavior." Tony looked Flo in the eyes. It seemed like he was talking to a child. "Don't flush any paper towels down the toilet.

Lou's done giving you chances," Tony called to Flo's back as she shuffled to the green door with her legs squeezed together.

"It's gonna take her forever to get all the pantyhose off," I said thinking aloud.

"What?" Tony asked.

"Flo wears seven pairs of pantyhose under her army pants. Do you know why?"

"Being on the street is hard. Especially for women. And especially for people like Flo. I imagine she's wearing all those layers to protect herself."

"Oh," I said. I understood about protecting yourself. "What do you mean 'people like Flo'?"

"Well, in case you haven't noticed, Flo's not all there upstairs." Tony tapped his hairy finger against his temple, and I nodded in agreement. He continued, "She showed up here at Naples about two years ago. I bet she's been on the street a lot longer."

"You're really nice to her."

"Sometimes we do for others what we can't do for our own." Tony brought his cigarette to his lips for a long time. A large cloud of smoke came out of Tony's mouth and he spoke again. "My brother went crazy after Nam. He lived on the streets, and not one of us could reach him. He died. Ran out in front of a moving car."

Tony sat on the wooden crate, but I could tell he was somewhere else. I felt bad about his brother, but now was the time to ask him for help. I didn't want Flo to know anything about my father, about me asking Tony for help, or anything about me.

So I lowered my voice to a whisper. "Can you help me? I need to get to Reidsville. My real father lives there. Do you know how I could get there?"

Tony leaned toward me and listened.

"I'm thinking I should take a bus or something. The truckers

I've asked to give me a ride aren't going there. 'Not on my route,' they all say."

"Well," Tony started with his head close to mine.

"Shhh." I brought my fingers to my mouth. "Flo's coming."

Flo came from the alley, which meant when she left the bathroom she'd walked through the restaurant. "Flo's coming," she mocked. Toilet paper dragged from both of her feet, and a wad of bathroom paper towels was stuffed under her armpit. Tony stood up, threw his cigarette down, and ground it out with his shoe.

"Flo, I told you never go *through* the restaurant. Dammit, I'm gonna get it now. Lou's probably red-faced and spitting nails. I gotta go and smooth it out." Tony grabbed the green door. "Lacy, come back tomorrow before lunch, and I'll help you with that problem. I've got an idea." As he opened the door, I heard a man's voice screaming, "Tony! Tony!"

Flo scurried to her spot along the wall, placed the napkins in one of her plastic bags, and whispered to the air. She sat down. I finished my last crumbs of chips, and Flo babbled in a high-pitched voice and looked up at the night sky. She kept repeating the same thing over and over. I couldn't understand the words. Her bottom lip came out, her forehead wrinkled, and she rocked side to side.

"Flo, are you okay?" She didn't answer. I asked her a second time. I stared at her, waiting for an answer. She looked like a child, a five-year-old. It was weird how someone as old as Flo could suddenly look so different. She began to hum. I recognized the song; it was from that Christmas ballet, the one where the snow fairies dance around. I had seen it on TV three years in a row. After a few minutes, the song faded and her body stopped rocking.

"Do you like Tony?" she asked, in her scratchy voice.

"Yeah, he's nice."

"He's *my* friend! He helps me!" Flo yelled. Her face became the same color as her nose, and she stared at me like we were in a blinking contest.

Finally, the contest was over and she reached for her half-eaten sandwich. Watching Flo eat a sandwich made me realize I wanted to keep all my teeth. It took forever for her to finish one bite. I wondered what Flo had been before? Had she run away as a child? Had she fought in some war and then gone crazy? Or had she been crazy all along? I threw my trash away and stared at Flo's face as she worked on chewing the last bite of her sandwich.

"Can I ask you a question, Flo?"

"Only if I can ask you two," she said still chewing.

"Okay. How long have you been on the street?" I asked, knowing I didn't have to answer her questions.

"Forever." She smiled and stood. Flo pulled her black knit hat over her red bushy hair and gathered her plastic bags. "My turn. Number one," she said making the number one sign with her dirty index finger. "Did your daddy like your pretty face? Is that why you left?"

"You don't know anything." I grabbed my duffel bag. Staring at me again, Flo smiled and sang, "Lacy's running away, 'cause she won't play. Lacy's got no home, where she can go. Lacy's gonna end up, just like ol' Flo!" She cackled and threw her head back.

"Shut up, Flo, just shut up."

I ran into the alley and put the strap of my bag over my head and across my chest. Flo followed behind me and spoke again, "I got one more question, Lacy."

"I'm not talking to you! You're a crazy old woman." I walked faster toward the end of the alley.

"You still sleeping at the stadium? Like I told you?" Flo shouted to my back.

Someone had stolen my last bed, so I grabbed some more cardboard boxes from the dumpster, stepped onto the sidewalk, and crossed the street. Flo didn't follow me, but I kept hearing her voice all the way to the stadium. Turning around a couple of times, I swore that she was right behind me.

6

"Hey, baby," a man said. I didn't move and pretended to be asleep. He leaned against the metal fence across from the bleachers and lit a cigarette. The end glowed red when he brought it to his mouth again. "Is your name Lacy?"

How did he know my name? I didn't answer and hoped he would go away. The fence rattled when his foot pushed off. He walked over and tapped the bottom of my shoe with his foot. "Are you Lacy?" he asked louder.

I pretended to be waking up and propped myself up on my elbow. He crouched down and the tips of his snakeskin boots touched my cardboard bed. The smell of sweat mixed with musky cologne smothered me. His arm reached for my shoulder. Because of the tightness of his leather jacket, his arm strained, and I moved away from its reach.

"No, I'm not Lacy."

"That's funny, you look just like Flo said Lacy would look." The man took a long drag of his cigarette and blew the smoke in my face. My heart pumped in my ears. He stood up and turned. I released the breath I had been holding. He flicked his cigarette deep under the bleachers, and with his back to me, he spoke again. "Do you know where I might find *Lacy*? Flo told me she'd be sleeping at the stadium. And me and Lacy, well, we've got a date."

The hairs on my neck rose. I scrambled to stand, and the soles of my shoes slipped against the cardboard. Before I could get to my feet, his fingers closed around my wrist. I tried to pull away, and he squeezed harder.

"Let me go." I tried to pry his fingers from my wrist. His face was covered in whiskers, and his nearly shaved head and sharp chin made his face look like a triangle. Tightening his grip, he placed my hand against his cheek, opened my fingers and rubbed my hand over his jawline.

I dug my fingernails into his skin.

He smiled. "Flo told me you were feisty. But she didn't tell me you'd be this much work." His hand reached back over his shoulder, and then I felt the sting. I moved back along the cardboard, trying to get away, but my wrist was trapped. With a jerk, he pulled me to him and squeezed my fingers, mashing them so hard I thought they were broken. He lifted my arm like I was a puppet and kissed my aching fingers.

"What do you want?" I asked, afraid of his answer.

"Flo and I have this arrangement. I give her what she wants, and she gives me what I want," he said, tracing my lips with his finger. "She told me you like older men, is that true?" His hand slid up my thigh. I kicked him between his legs. He fell backward and released my wrist. I ran. At the last bleacher, his arm hooked around my neck—my teeth tried to find his flesh, but his leather armor was too thick—and he pulled me back to the cardboard bed.

He threw me down and pressed my shoulders into the ground. I screamed and kicked my legs. With my arms and hands, I hit and scratched his face, trying to find his eyes with my fingernails. As if he were riding a horse, he straddled my chest and grabbed my wrists. It was hard to breathe. He licked a line from my chin to my forehead. The hairs from his face sliced my cheek, and his taste of cigarettes and alcohol was on my lips. I closed my eyes. "Open your eyes, you little bitch." Above my face, he held one of my arms. "Are you hot for me now?" he asked, holding his lighter under the palm of my hand, burning my skin. He squeezed his legs against me, pinning my arms against my body; his long cold fingers crawled up my shirt. I threw my head from side to side and tried to buck my body free. With one quick blow of his fist, my head fell, and I couldn't see for a moment.

A sharp pain hit my jaw and blood filled my mouth. My head tingled. "Oh Lacy, this should've been so much easier," I heard him say as his fist rose again in the air.

"RUN! RUN! I GOT HIM!" someone yelled. Away from the bleachers, near what looked like a concession stand, I saw two men wrestling with each other. I didn't know the second man, but I recognized the snakeskin boots that stuck out from the human pile. I stood up quickly, and then fell back to the ground. The bleachers seemed to be moving. I closed my eyes, rolled myself onto my hands and knees and waited for the spinning to stop. Slowly, I brought myself up to standing.

"Run! I can't hold him forever," the guy on top shouted at me. I grabbed my bag and hobbled away. As my head adjusted to being upright, I picked up speed and ran all the way to Naples restaurant. I banged on the green door and called for Tony. No one answered.

"It's too late for food." Flo's scratchy voice came from the darkness.

"Where are you, Flo?"

"Over here." Flo staggered out from the building behind Naples. She had a half empty bottle of Jim Beam clutched to her chest. "Did he get there in time? My friend?" Her free hand reached for the brick wall to steady herself. "I just wanted a little juice," she slurred and presented the bottle by the neck to me. "I was thirsty, that's all. Me and Boots have this deal. I give him what he wants, and he gives me juice."

"What?" A fire swept over me, the kind of fire that burns acres of forest like kindling. I pushed Flo against the wall, holding her shoulders just like Boots had held mine minutes before.

"I was almost raped!" I yelled into her face. "And for what? Just because you were thirsty?" The bottle clinked against the wall as I shook her shoulders. With her chin toward her chest, she didn't try to get free. Instead of fighting me, she went limp. I stopped shaking her, but dug my fingers into her upper arms. Her sky eyes framed in rippled skin locked with mine.

"I'm sorry, Lacy." She looked away. With one final push, I let her go. Flo lost her balance and fell to the ground. She lifted the bottle to her lips and drank. She couldn't hold all that she had taken, and the liquid flowed from the corners of her mouth onto her coat. "He'll come looking for you," she said and wiped her mouth with the back of her hand.

"Why, Flo?"

"'Cause a deal's a deal."

"No, why did you set me up? What have I done to you to make you hate me?" I leaned into her face.

"Hate you?" she laughed. "I don't hate you. I like you. Why do you think I sent my friend to stop Boots?" She looked at me like I should thank her. The fire burned again inside me.

"Like me! Dammit Flo, I don't want you to *like* me!" Flo's head hung down, I wondered if she had passed out. With my palm on her forehead, I pushed her head back and yelled into her face, "I was almost raped because of you!"

I spun around. I couldn't even look at her. My fists balled at my sides. When I turned back, Flo had scooted away from me. Her face changed from an old woman's to a child's, and she curled herself around the Jim Beam bottle and began to hum that song again.

"Oh my God, you're so crazy!" I kicked some trash at her.

In a small voice she said, "Boots'll come looking for both of us. He'll be *mad,* and he won't stop, a deal's a deal."

"I'm not yours—you can't give me away!"

"Don't matter. I already did."

I didn't have the energy to argue with Flo. I left her in the alley with her juice. I wasn't going to let Boots get me again. I had to hide, but I just wanted to sleep. I walked in the opposite direction of the stadium and hoped Fifth Street would lead me out of the city. All the way down the street, I kept hearing *a deal's a deal,* Samuel Mitchell yelling, my mother crying, and a constant ringing.

My body ached. I couldn't go on, not another step.

Almost at the end of Fifth Street, I found a spot behind a motorcycle shop. To hide myself, I pushed two trash cans slightly out from the building and slid myself close to the wall. I curled up in a ball, placed my bag on top of me, and fell into a deep sleep.

WHEN I AWOKE, the sun was high in the sky. The voices were gone, but the ringing in my head was still there. As I started a yawn, my jaw tightened. Gently, I placed my fingers on the pain —a golf ball had grown on my jaw overnight. I picked the bits of dried blood off my lips, sat up, and looked around. On the back of my hands were scratches that looked like road maps and black strips of dirt were underneath my nails. The world started to spin. I threw up and wiped my mouth with my sleeve.

Stretched thinly across the blue sky were high white clouds, and the birds talked to each other. The sun beat down on me and the garbage in the cans. Sardines, tuna—it had to be some kind of fish, I couldn't tell—or whatever it was, the smell made me want to throw up again. I slid my back against the wall, steadied myself, and picked up my bag. From underneath the bag, a group of cockroaches scurried away. They moved so fast I couldn't tell if they were American or German. That was another thing I liked about cockroaches—their names. Even their scientific order name, Blattaria—which means to shun light—was interesting.

The ringing in my head sounded just like those Madagascar hissing cockroaches that I'd seen in a traveling display at school. That was when I fell in love with insects. It must have been second grade. All the girls had squirmed around the glass tank that held the shiny roaches and the boys pushed the most frightened girls toward the tank again and again. I guarded my spot close to the tank. I hadn't had time for their stupid games—I was entranced. The woman giving the talk said something that made me appreciate those roaches more than people. She said, "Both the males and females seem to care for the young nymphs." She showed us a picture and continued, "Can you see the nymphs underneath the male? Before this picture was shot, we disturbed the nymphs and they ran under the adult male. He let them stay there and protected them with his body." I remember thinking at the time, it would be great to be a Madagascar hissing cockroach.

I walked away from the city and toward a hope of finding my real father.

7

A bout two hours into my walking, buildings started to get farther away from each other, and small houses shaped like squares appeared. In a dumpster in the back of a Roses Discount Store, I found lunch: a half-eaten pack of cheese crackers and a half-empty bottle of Coke. As I walked through the neighborhoods, I looked around and watched the people. An old man in plaid shorts washing his car stared at me. His face and nose squeezed tight, like he had tasted something sour. He stopped washing his car and inspected me as I walked by his house. Maybe he thought I was going to steal something, but the only thing around was a kid's Big Wheel on the sidewalk. I stepped around the three-wheel toy, turned my head, and gave him a smile and a wave. He shook his head and went back to washing his car.

I walked and counted the number of cracks in the sidewalk. It was amazing how many there were. My legs got tired, but I knew I had to make the most of the daylight. At 257, I stopped counting. It just seemed dumb to keep going, and to tell the truth, I kept forgetting the number of the last crack I had counted.

My favorite cracks were the ones made by trees; their roots busted out and took back their space from the sidewalk. Sometimes if the tree roots were big enough, they made concrete mountains. I thought about how people could look normal on the outside and still have something waiting to bust out of them.

When other people were around, my mother had pretended she was normal and that everything was fine. But when she was alone and thought no one was looking, she would cry. Samuel Mitchell had acted differently when people were around too. Some weekends, especially in the summer, his welder friends would over, and both my mother and father had acted like we were a perfect family. My mother laughed at all the funny things my father said—not because she thought they were funny, but because she knew she had to. Samuel would kiss her and pull her onto his lap. He did this not because he loved her, but because he wanted all his friends to know she was his.

A SMALL SLICE of the moon showed. Night was here, and I needed somewhere to stay. Somewhere safe. A church sign, a cross with a red flame, was lit up across the street. I remembered my mother taking me to a church like this one when I was around five. It was Easter, and I'd worn a red dress with navy blue curvy trim that my mother had made for me. She'd twisted my hair in a bun on the top of my head. When I twirled, the bottom of the dress spun out like an umbrella, and my mother had smiled. The people at the church were friendly toward my mother and let me hunt eggs with the other children.

The doors of the church were dark, glossy wood, and the shiny gold handles caught the light from the street lamp. I pulled on the handle and the door opened. At first, I expected to see all the people from that Easter. But there was no one. The front area was dark and quiet. Papers, posters, and pictures hung on the walls. And it smelled old—old like our basement. I slowly walked farther into the building and waited for someone to throw me out.

My mother and I never had been inside any church. It was so quiet except for a humming sound. I walked over a metal vent, and cool air circled around me. Inside the large room, it was dark. After a few moments, my eyes adjusted. I stood in the back of the room. The ceiling was high and shaped like an oval dome. Long wooden benches were on each side of the center aisle.

I walked up the center aisle, letting my finger ride over the tops of each wooden bench. The carpet was a deep burnt red, and the bench cushions matched the carpet. As I got closer, I noticed a gold cross on the front of the minister's stand. In the center of the wall above the stage area, a cross hung. It was just two pieces of wood. There was no Jesus. Where was the Jesus? All crosses are supposed to have a Jesus.

I pretended to be the minister and spoke into the microphone, "Someone has stolen our Jesus." I pointed behind me to the empty cross. I could hear the people gasp. "And I know you people know who did it. So, please come and confess to me in your confession after I'm done. Thanks for being here today. Amen." I stood there waiting for the guilty person to step forward and tell me what they did with Jesus. But before I could hear any confessions, a light came on in the hallway.

I hid behind the piano.

"Did you get the trash from the classrooms?" a woman asked.

"Yeah," a man's voice replied. He started to whistle.

"What about the bathrooms? Last time, you forgot the women's bathroom trash."

He sighed, stopped his song, and said, "I got it already. Let's lock up and go get something to eat."

"Did you dust the altar? The pastor called me about the dust and trash in the sanctuary last week. Do *I* need to check behind you?"

"Nooooo," he said, his voice speaking like the woman. After a moment of silence he said, "All right, Jo. I'll quadruple check it."

The whistling man came into the room, turned on a few lights, stopped at the beginning of the benches—nowhere near where a minister would be—and waited for a moment.

"Yeah, it's dust free, just like I told you. Now let's go eat."

"Check under the pews. Kids leave food under there," the woman's voice sounded muffled. The man gave a sigh and set down a bucket. His keys jingled as he bent down and sometimes the metal collection hit against the wood benches. He worked his way from the back to the front of each side.

By the time he reached the first pew of the other side, he groaned when his body hunched over, allowing his eyes to see under the bench. After the last bench, I breathed a little easier. The whistling began again, and he was on his way out. When he stopped and stared at the altar, I tried to think of a reason for me to be there, something that would seem sensible but most important, believable. Nothing came to me. Maybe the blow to my head had effected my brain. I didn't want to go back outside, and I knew that if he found me, he'd kick me out.

He walked up the center aisle, and I tucked myself close to the back of the piano.

I heard things being removed off the altar. A snap like that of a clean sheet being shook out for folding made me jump. I closed my eyes tight and hoped that I hadn't made any noise. The man whistled his song again. I opened my eyes, expecting to see his face peering at me. Something clattered and the man cursed.

"Where'd you go?" the man said. As he spoke the word *go*, a long white candle came rolling beside my feet. I pushed the candle with my feet to the edge of the piano. I scooted back again, close to the piano. His fingers stretched out against the carpet and searched the floor. His keys slapped against the piano.

"I got you!" he said and grabbed the candle. He sat down and his backside was at my feet.

"I'm too old for this," he said and wiped his forehead with a white cloth.

"What's the holdup in there? Do you want to go eat?" the woman said at the doorway of the room. The man let out a long bear roar, grabbed onto the piano's edge, and pulled himself upright.

The switches flipped again, taking away the light, and I heard the man's bucket hit the hallway's hard floor. In a few trips, they had moved their cleaning supplies outside of the church, and the hallway light went off. I heard the keys jingle against the handle of the outside of the door.

Locked in. I decided that the church was not a bad place to be locked in. It was a lot better than the stadium. The darkness surrounded me again. I crawled under the first bench, stretched, and realized how tired I was. Without moving from under the bench, I slid my bag above my head. My eyes burned. The space between the floor and the bottom of the bench was just enough for me; so, not by choice, I slept on my back.

IN THE EARLY MORNING, I dreamed I was a trapeze artist. On a platform high above the crowd, I stood, waiting for my introduction. The ringleader came to the center of the ring and yelled into his megaphone, "And now for your enjoyment, The Amazing Moth Girl." My costume—a rust-colored bodysuit with paper-like wings that glittered brown, black, and white—felt open and cool air tickled my back. I stood frozen in fear. The leader announced me again, someone behind me zipped the bodysuit closed and whispered in my ear, "It's okay."

I placed my hands on the bar and floated into the air. The crowd marveled at me. And then, I was flying without the trapeze. I spun, dived, and sliced through the air. When I landed in front of the audience, my wings were covered with hundreds of live tulip-tree moths. Mesmerized by the moths, I didn't see the fire-eater come into the ring and begin his act. He blew fire from his mouth onto a long rod and waved it around the air, preparing to eat the fire. The rod touched my left hand, burning it and setting the skin on fire. I jumped at the pain, and when I did, all of the moths flew away. I chased them, not caring that my hand was on fire. I wanted them to come back to me.

I opened my eyes. During the night, my left arm had stretched out from under the bench. Through a high window, a ray of sunshine beamed on my palm. I jerked my hand back under the bench, glad it wasn't really on fire. The skin, blistered and raw where Boots had burned me, hurt. I blew on my palm and rolled out from underneath the bench.

In the dark last night, I couldn't see him. But with the light shining, he was there. And not only one Jesus, but two. Beside the cross, on either side, were painted-glass pictures of him. The one on the left was of Jesus praying, his elbows resting on a big rock. The picture on the right was Jesus in a white robe with his hair blown back. He reminded me of the girls in the shampoo commercials.

Clapping and loud whistles came from the back of the room. Were the people I had imagined last night back? I slowly stood to get a better look. But there was no one. Again, the clapping and whistles. I smelled coffee, and with coffee, there could be food. My stomach growled.

I went out of the room with the benches. Near the front doors, I heard someone talking. Holding onto the railing, I eased down a flight of old steps. When I reached the bottom, I saw about twenty people sitting in metal folding chairs facing each other. One person stood; it was his voice I had followed down the stairs. He took a bow and sat down. Everyone clapped and whistled.

A blonde woman rose from her chair. Her shoulders were like a man's, but her chest filled out the blue button-down shirt in a way no man could. She looked my way. I moved against the wall and out of sight.

8

"My name is Annie, and I'm an alcoholic," the blonde woman said. Her voice was deep for a woman, but it sounded smooth like syrup running over a stack of pancakes. My stomach roared again. I leaned over so I could see her, but not far enough where she could see me. Annie's blonde shoulder-length hair was tied in a loose ponytail, and she wore no makeup. "But on June thirteenth, I will celebrate my eleventh birthday party! No cake, thank you. Just my chip, please," Annie said and laughed.

Again, everyone burst into clapping and whistling. The guy who spoke first must have been the leader because he looked at everyone and asked if anyone was ready to share. About five people from the circle of metal chairs stood and told their stories. A skinny man across the circle from Annie got the loudest clap. He'd had the shortest time without alcohol—six months. Of the faces I could see, I watched them as they said their names and talked about drinking. Some of them used their hands when they spoke, some looked up at the ceiling, some looked down, and some cried, but there was pain on all of their faces.

A woman with long brown hair sat with her back to me. She didn't speak. The leader asked a couple of times if there was anyone else who wanted to share. After a long time of silence, he sat down and said, "Ken's—"

"I don't drink," the woman blurted out. "It's my husband. I didn't know what else to do. Except to come here."

"We're glad you came," Annie said.

"He just won't stop, nothing I say helps, and he shuts me out now, all the time." Her voice cracked. "I don't know what to do anymore."

The leader walked to the table and poured some coffee in a cup, he pointed to the sugar and creamer. The woman shook her head no. He brought to it her and said, "It's good you came, welcome." He sat back down in his chair and continued, "Ken was supposed to be a guest speaker tonight, but he had a family emergency. Annie, would you mind?"

"Nope, you know I don't mind talking," she said as she placed her coffee cup on the floor. "I remember my first sponsor. He was ex-military and a hoot. He'd tell me, 'Annie, you've got to have the three D's to beat the enemy.' The enemy. I had never thought of alcohol as the enemy before, it had always been my friend, my close friend. You know what I mean, right?" Annie shifted in her chair and reached for her coffee.

"The first D, I think, is the hardest. It's Decision. The decision to give it up. My life with Gin and Ray was very different than the one I have now. Gin of course, my liquor of choice, and Ray, my alcoholic husband. Ray and I were successful—he was a bank manager and I was a loan officer. Not at the same bank. We met in the banking circles. We had been married for about three years—and by the way, we were great together when we were sober—and I got pregnant. We were both so excited about having a baby. Lowell Charles Smith, our beautiful baby son, came into the world on June 13 and six weeks later, he died. I put my baby to bed, and in the morning, he was gone." Annie hung her head down. She picked up her cup, and her fingers traced around the outside of the cup. I couldn't see if she was crying, but everyone looked in Annie's direction, waiting for her to continue. The skinny man rubbed his face, like he was trying to wipe away Annie's words.

"The loss sent Ray and I spiraling down. And when we got to the bottom, we drank. We drank to stop feeling, and we drank to live. For six years this went on. By the seventh year, we both had lost our jobs." Annie went to the table, took a white pitcher with a stained spout, and moved around the center of the chairs, refilling the empty cups.

The step I kneeled on started to dig into my knees. I shifted, and my flashlight fell out of my bag. It didn't fall down the steps but made a loud clink. I waited. The bathrooms were across from the steps; if they hadn't heard the flashlight, it would be just a matter of time before someone came this way, if they weren't already. I decided the next time there was clapping or any noise, I'd creep back up the stairs.

Annie's voice started again. "Once, on a binge, Ray pointed a gun at me and asked if I wanted to stop living. He said he would shoot me then himself. After I told him not to shoot me, he placed the gun under his chin ... he couldn't pull the trigger. I walked away hoping he would shoot me in the back." Annie sat back in her chair and closed her eyes. She laced her fingers and cradled the back of her head with her hands. The man next to Annie patted her shoulder, and a metal chair screeched against the floor as the longhaired woman got up for more coffee. I should've left the church, but I wanted to hear Annie. She had wanted to die—I knew that feeling. I switched positions, sat on my bottom, pulling my knees into my chest, and tried to be quiet.

Samuel had never pulled a gun on me or my mother. He'd

used things you didn't think of as weapons. Belts, paddles, brooms, and his hands. The Ping-Pong paddle with the drilled holes hurt the worst. Or maybe, the paddle hurt the most because I was still young and hadn't taught myself not to cry. I let my head fall against the cool cement wall, closed my eyes, and listened to Annie.

"Then, money got tight. Ray starting sleeping around with anyone who would buy him booze. I found a part-time job bartending. Always keeping my candy close." She paused and I heard the skinny man say, "Yeah."

"My parents died that same year," Annie's voice continued. "Some days, I never got out of bed, and a bottle of gin was my nourishment for the day. At my parents' funeral, I met my brother's wife, Ginger. *Gin*ger. I think God has a wicked sense of humor. She was a recovering alcoholic and suggested I go with her to a meeting. Even though I tried to hide my drinking from my brother, and everyone else, my little brother knew. And he told his wife, and she, knowing rock bottom herself, took me on as her mission." Annie laughed. I leaned to the edge of the wall again and stared at Annie. She pushed the blonde strands that had escaped from her ponytail back and away from her face.

She looked in my direction and spoke again. "I went to that first meeting thinking I had no problem. I was *just a little depressed*, and who wouldn't be with my loss, I told myself. I tried to stop many times. Each failure made me feel more like drinking. Ginger didn't give up on me. That's the second D—Determination. That comes from inside you, and the determination of those around you. Finally, on Lowell's birthday the next year I stopped drinking. And I stopped for good ... well, I stopped for that day. And then a week went by, and then it was a month and now look, it's going to be eleven years. And that's the third D— Discipline. Oh my God, it's hard work staying sober. But it's worth it .... I'm living now, not hiding." Annie was silent for a few moments. "Thanks for listening."

She unfolded from her chair and walked back to the table and placed her cup down. Everyone clapped. She swept the table with her hands and brushed the spilled sugar into her cup. As she gathered the trash on the table, she stared at the wall that I was behind. It seemed like she could see right through the wall —like how those x-ray glasses I sent away for should've worked. I moved up two steps.

"Folks, I was so long-winded, I know some of you are dying for a smoke. The church doesn't allow smoking in the building, so the back parking lot is a great spot for a smoke break. Please take a doughnut with you, they're very good!" Annie said. Over the noise of the moving metal chairs, Annie spoke again, almost yelling, "And we'll *all* be going outside for the break. Make sure to get yourself a jelly doughnut to enjoy."

I didn't know for sure if she knew I was behind the wall, but I decided her invitation for doughnuts was for me too. The door shut behind them, and I ran to the table and took three dough-nuts and a cup of coffee. I didn't drink coffee, but I was thirsty. I went up the stairs back to the room with the benches. It seemed to me that this would be a room well used in a church. So, I decided to look for something more private. I balanced my doughnuts and coffee and crept up another set of steps that led to another floor of the church. Down at the end of a hallway, there was a closet with brooms, mops, buckets, and various ladders. Inside, I dropped my bag and placed the glazed treats on top.

A table. That's what I needed. So, I turned a bucket over, wiped the spiderwebs off the bottom with my sleeve, and put my coffee down on the table. In the ceiling was a light bulb with a long string hanging down, I pulled and there was light. I shut the door for privacy, wrapped my legs around the bucket and let each doughnut dissolve in my mouth slowly. The bitter coffee made the doughnuts taste all the sweeter.

I licked each finger and looked around. It was a big closet—a couple of hammers hung on the walls, a beat-up vacuum cleaner sat on top of a wood pile, and webs of extension cords tangled at the bottom of the ladders. Until I could figure out what to do next, I needed a place to stay and the closet, with a little rearranging, would be perfect. I didn't want to meet Tommy Franco looking like a zombie. After a few weeks, the bruises and cuts would be gone, and then I'd find Tommy Franco. I wanted him to see me, not what Boots had done.

A RUMBLING of voices came from below. I put my ear down on the floor and heard the voices from downstairs saying the same thing together.

"God, grant me the serenity to accept the things I cannot change, the courage to change the things I can, and the wisdom to know the difference." I then heard clapping and metal chairs being moved.

At the time, I had no idea the words were a prayer. *Courage* was the only word I could remember when the voices stopped, but my mind went to its opposite: fear. I thought about Flo being afraid of Boots, about her seven pairs of pantyhose, and how she'd traded me to Boots for alcohol. I thought about Annie, her husband, and their dead baby, even though she didn't act like it when she told her story, I wondered if she'd been afraid to die when her husband pointed the gun at her. I thought about my mother and Samuel Mitchell. My mother lived in fear, always afraid of what Samuel would say or do, and when she drank, sometimes the fear would leave her. Pain and drinking are partners, I decided. Everyone in that room (and everyone I knew) had some kind of trouble caused by drinking.

Saturday mornings, my mother and I had waited in the car for Samuel Mitchell as he went into the ABC store. When I was in kindergarten, I used to think he went in to buy letters, like the letters of the alphabet. When Samuel came back to the car, my mother hid the brown bags right away at her feet. By first grade, I'd figured out what was inside the brown bags, and if there was more than one bag, I knew it was best for me to stay out of their way for the weekend. Those weekends turned into my insect hunts. If it didn't rain, I stayed outside all day and searched for dead bugs. At first, I'd collected them in jelly jars. As I got older, I'd pinned them to cardboard and hung them on my walls. Samuel hated my collections. He'd complained about dead bugs being on the walls and how it wasn't right for a girl to have things like that. I don't know why he let me keep them.

Once, when I still kept my bugs in jars, he tried to add to my collection.

"Hey, Lacybug, come here," he called. The last two words slurred together, and it was only lunchtime. But when he called me Lacybug, I knew he was in a good mood. It was safe. In the living room, on the table beside him, was a glass bottle that looked like a man. The bottle's cap was a wide brimmed hat.

"I got a bug for your collection, gimme your hand."

"Okay." I held out my hand.

He placed a fat white worm in the palm of my hand. It was cold and wet. I stared at it. I didn't know at the time it was an agave worm, which, if left alone to live in Mexico—instead of being drowned in alcohol—would become a butterfly.

"Eat it," he said.

"I don't eat my bugs, Daddy." A puddle of liquid had formed underneath the worm and my hand trembled.

"Eat it. It taste like chicken."

I shook my head no.

He yelled, "Eat the goddamn thing."

My mother must have heard him because she stepped beside me and said, "For God's sake, Samuel, leave her alone."

He grabbed the worm out of my hand and put it into his mouth, chewing so I could see. "Chicken, it tastes just like chicken." He leaned back in his chair and closed his eyes.

My mother whispered in my ear, "Go outside and play." All day, my hand had smelled like alcohol, and I'd seen that white worm everywhere.

I lifted my head off the floor. I had fallen asleep. Below me was quiet. I looked around again at the closet, my new house. In one corner, there were some connected wide boards painted with green grass and smiling flowers. I stood and searched for a hiding place. From behind the boards, I moved about fifty paint cans, some were full and some were almost empty with dried paint rivers running down the sides. And when I was done, there was a cleared area almost big enough for me to lie down. I got into my space and stacked the empty buckets on top of the paint cans. If anyone came into the closet, they wouldn't even know I was there.

After a week at the church, I knew the schedule. Saturday mornings, doughnuts from the AA meetings. Early Sunday mornings, the men of the church made a breakfast, and that meant the possibility of bacon and eggs. It was so easy to sneak into the kitchen while the men ate their food and talked about the church and sports.

During the day, I stayed in the closet, sleeping and reading my field guide. Monday through Friday from midmorning until lunchtime, the hallway was filled with the little voices of preschool kids. The best part of the preschool was their refrigerator—lots of foods to choose from, but I never took a lot of one thing.

The women of the church met every Friday in a room across from my closet. There were always some leftovers thrown in the room's trash can when they were done. The minister worked from midmorning until early afternoon. The toughest people to hide from were the cleaning people. They came every Friday night. When they were in the building, I stayed in the closet.

My clothes smelled and needed to be washed. So, after figuring out the safest day and the safest time, I did laundry on Tuesdays at midnight. I used the two sinks in the bathrooms, one filled with soap and water and the other to rinse. As I scrubbed, I noticed in the mirror the bruises on my face were green and purple with yellow outlines. My hair had grown a couple of inches, but it still stuck out all over my head. Hair cutting was not one of my best skills.

I went back to the closet to hang my clean wet clothes. Gray paint oozed under the door and formed a puddle on the light blue carpet in the hallway. When I had left with my dirty clothes, I tripped over a paint can and kicked it with my foot. The can rolled across the floor of the closet, but I hadn't noticed that a second can had tipped over and emptied. I threw the clothes across the wooden boards and ran back to the bathroom for napkins and a plastic bag.

Hard paint rocks floated in the sea of gray, and the paint dripped long icicles as my hand moved from the floor to the trash bag. It took me two hours to clean the mess. I tried my best to get the gray out of the carpet, but there was a light gray half-circle that looked like a permanent welcome mat. I placed the bag full of the soaked napkins underneath some other trash in the outside dumpster.

The cool night air was a nice change from being inside. On the cement porch outside the back door, I lay on my back and stared at the night sky, looking for the Big Dipper. I found it using the two pointing stars. I saw the North Star. In history class, I remembered learning about the ancient sailors who used the North Star to guide them as they sailed across oceans to follow their dreams.

The North Star wasn't even the brightest, but because it stayed in one place in the sky everyone could depend on it. I liked that. With my face almost healed, I needed a plan, a plan to find Tommy Franco, and the stars weren't going to work for me.

A map. The church library would have one. All libraries should have maps, I reasoned. I was in Cherryville and that was southwest of Reidsville. If I was going to walk or hitch, I needed to know which roads, and this time I'd make sure I didn't fall asleep.

The next evening, I picked the lock of the library. It was on the main level with the sanctuary. I flicked on the light and searched for a map. Two huge copy machines took up most of the space, so there wasn't a lot of room for the number of books that a library should have. I never knew there were so many types of Bibles, and there were no books on insects, I checked. Stashed between two bookcases was a tall book with the word *Atlas* on the binding. I sat down, pulled it out, and dusted the cobwebs off the cover. When it was clean, I could read the title: *The Atlas of Biblical Times.*

"Someone left the light on again in the library." A hand reached into the room, turned the light off, and shut the library door.

I froze.

"No one around here thinks about how much the electric bill is each month," the woman's voice continued.

Through the glass that bordered the door on either side, I saw two old women. One was fat and the other skinny. The skinny one's hair was so tall. Actually, it looked like a beehive. If a good wind ever came along, she would've blown away. The heavy woman's hair was blue. The top of her hair peaked and the ends flipped out; it looked like a bell.

"Can you believe that Peggy Lynn is heading up vacation

bible school this year?" said the Bluebell. Not giving the Beehive a chance to answer she continued. "I'll tell you what, it will be a disaster. How will we reach the sinners in our community with such an unorganized person in charge? Peggy can't even keep up with her own family!"

Beehive nodded and Bluebell continued. "Have you heard about the Italian supper?" Not even taking a breath, Bluebell spoke again, her face red from lack of air. "Every year, I make the spaghetti sauce. Every year! In ten years, I've never gotten one bad review. Everybody loves my sauce. Personally, I think it's why the people come back. What do you think?"

"Your sauce is good, but—"

Bluebell started again. "That Annie is having the thing catered. The women of the church enjoy cooking. Annie said she wanted to 'give us women a break.' She said, she wanted everyone to enjoy themselves. Ha, I think she enjoys telling us what to do! I don't know why Phyllis isn't arranging the spaghetti supper. Do you? And, Annie wants to invite the community? Do you know how much that is going to cost the church? Offering free catered meals! It would be one thing if we, the women of the church, had cooked the food."

"We're going be late to the meeting. It's in the sanctuary, right? Remember, Phyllis's husband has cancer and Annie was the only one who volunteered to be in charge of the supper. Remember?" Beehive said to Bluebell as they walked away.

MY BRUISES WERE JUST a faint yellow. It was time to find Tommy, but I had never found a map anywhere in the church. Not even in the church's office. I went into the sanctuary to plunk the piano keys; it helped me think. It was Tuesday night, which meant no meetings, no cleaning people, no Boy Scouts, and no blue-haired old ladies.

I gazed at the clipping of Tommy Franco and reread the letter. From my folding and unfolding, the clipping started to rip in the creases. In the blurry black-and-white photo, he was smiling, and I imagined him and my mother in the photo booth getting their picture taken. She'd probably sat with her legs draped over his, they'd laughed and maybe she'd tickled him. That was what made him move his head when the machine snapped the photo. I liked the thought about my mother tickling him, but it didn't seem true, not like the things I'd imagined about Tommy. In the clipping photo, I could only see his profile. I decided that the basketball he was shooting—which was caught in midair by the camera—definitely went in the basket. Why hadn't my mother married him? He loved her. And she must have loved him. She had kept all these things. Why hadn't she gone to him?

I folded the letter and clipping and placed them on top of the piano. The keys felt cold underneath my fingers. When I pushed the keys on one side, the music sounded angry, and I thought of Samuel Mitchell. Did she *choose* Samuel over Tommy? If she did, she was sorry. On the other end of the piano, the keys made music like fairies stepping on bells. I'd gotten away from Samuel Mitchell, but my mother was still there. Did she want to leave? Maybe she had already left. Maybe she was out looking for me.

I took my clipping and letter and moved from the piano to the front bench. The more I thought about my mother leaving or looking for me, the more I knew she didn't and wasn't. My mother reminded me of that clown I'd gotten for my eighth birthday. It was a blow-up clown as tall as me. The bottom was weighted and wider than the top, so when I punched it on the red nose, it always came back to me for another punch. She was like that with Samuel Mitchell. Why didn't she fight back? Not by hitting him, but by leaving him.

"Ahem." Someone cleared his throat in the back of the sanctuary. I turned around to see the minister. His white hair and beard looked like snow sprinkled with bits of road tar. From the collar of his red shirt, tufts of white chest hair stuck out. I hadn't seen him this close before. He walked toward me.

"What are you doing here?" I asked. When the words left my mouth, I knew it was a stupid question.

"I work here. I'm the pastor. Pastor Kurt is what everyone calls me." He walked up the aisle and stood at the end of my bench. "I'm meeting with a young couple tonight. They're getting married next month. Your turn—what are you doing here?"

"I, I ... I'm praying for my mom." Not exactly praying, I thought, but I had been thinking of her just before he had come in. That was close to the truth.

"That's great. I'd like to pray for your mother too. What's her name?" he said and sat down next to me on the bench.

"Justine," I said, not believing that I'd just given her real name. Maybe it was because he was the minister that I told him the truth.

"Justine, what a lovely name. What should I pray about Justine?" he said and looked at me. A large wooden cross hung from his neck. A name was fine, but I couldn't tell him what to pray for about my mother, so I looked at the carpet in front of me.

"I know. How about we close our eyes, and you say a prayer for your mother."

"Out loud?" I asked.

"Well, only if you want to. But you know, God knows what's in your heart. So, you can speak it out loud or say it silently to yourself. Either way works for me."

"How will you know what you're praying for?" I said.

"I'll pray for God to hear your prayer. And I'll pray for Justine and you. Can I have your name?"

"Lacy," I said, lacing my fingers together like the Jesus with his elbows on the rock. I closed my eyes. I wasn't sure what to say to myself. My mother's face came into my head. *I am sorry for running away, but I had to. Amen.* I opened my eyes and the minister was still praying, so I said, "Amen" out loud and he opened his eyes.

"Lacy, we are having an Italian spaghetti supper on Friday. I would love it if you would come. You'd be my guest."

"Uh, this Friday? Yeah ... I think I can make it," I said.

"Great! I've got to get to my office and get ready for my meeting," he said, looking at me like I should go home.

"I'm going to stay and pray for my mom some more, if that's all right."

"Sure, just let yourself out," he said and walked slowly down the aisle. He turned around in the middle of the sanctuary, one hand on his beard. He held the other hand in the air, flipped it back and forth, and examined it. His fingers combed downward against his beard and he said, "Do you like to paint?"

"Yeah," I said and wondered why he would ask me that. I looked down at my hands. From the spill, paint had pocketed itself under my fingernails and gray blotches still clung to my skin. I answered him, the first sentence tripped out of my mouth. "My parents and I are painting our porch, and I helped a few days ago. I've been trying to get it off, but it won't come off. That's why I'm here, for my mother. She fell off the ladder and broke her arm. Broke it in three places. She's in a cast now, that's why I had to help paint."

By the end of my excuse, words ran together, and I had to take a deep breath. I wondered if he bought it. If I had only had time to think about the story, prepare, my excuse would have been so much better. When Pastor Kurt smiled and walked away, I was sure he must have believed me.

"It was nice meeting you, Lacy. See you Friday. Oh, and bring your parents too." He walked down the main level hall and into his office. When I heard his office door close, I ran to my closet.

9

On Friday afternoon, as the preschool kids lined up in the hallway, the teachers discussed the "heat wave," and according to them, the hot temperatures and lack of rain was supposed to last another week. When their voices were in sanctuary, I slipped out of the closet and down the steps to the bottom level of the church. I wanted to make sure I looked like everybody else attending the spaghetti supper. As I stepped outside, the heat slammed into me like a moving wall.

When it had been hot like this at home, my mother used to say it was "hotter than forty hells." Once, I'd tried to fry an egg on the neighbor's blacktop driveway—I'd gotten in trouble for wasting an egg and even bigger trouble for the mess. About a week ago, when I'd been looking for a store, I found a school. It had a blacktop with a pole in the middle, and a swing set, merry-go-round, and seesaw in a grassy area.

I walked along the road to the school. The hot air made it hard to breathe and by the time I reached the playground, sweat ran off my body in little streams. Too tired and hot to move, I found a huge oak tree and sat down. I stayed under the oak all afternoon and watched ants shuttle up and down the bark.

Later, when it was close to dinnertime, I headed back to the church. The gravel parking lot was filled with cars. It seemed like the whole town was at the spaghetti dinner. On the sidewalk leading to the front doors, people lingered and talked with one another. Pastor Kurt shook the hands of everyone going in, hugged the old ladies, and patted the kids on their heads.

"Lacy," Pastor Kurt called to me. I walked over to the front doors. He reached for my hand to shake it. His other hand topped our hands, and he squeezed gently. "I'm so glad you could make it. Did your parents come with you?"

"No, they were too busy."

"Painting?"

"Yeah," I said and tucked my hands into the back pockets of my shorts.

"How's your mother's leg?"

"Her leg?"

"The one she broke in three places."

"Oh, you mean her arm. It's doing much better. The doctor said it's healing nicely."

"Yes, that's right, you did say it was her arm." Pastor Kurt smiled. "Well, I'm glad *you* weren't too busy. Come on in and have some supper."

I followed the crowd. They trickled down the old steps to the bottom level. People, tables, and chairs packed the room. The family in front of me stopped and a line formed. As I waited, I scanned the room. It looked so alive with the decorations and the people. Red-and-white checkered plastic tablecloths covered the surfaces, glass vases with one red flower and lots of green leaves were in the center of each table, music played from a radio in the corner, green, red, and white paper honeycomb balls hung from the ceiling, and people talked and smiled at one another like they hadn't seen each other in a long time.

When I reached the table with the food, I grabbed a plate of noodles. "Do you want meatballs?" a woman behind the table asked me. I answered yes, and she plopped three on top of my spaghetti.

"Could I have more?" I asked, and the woman stared at me.

"I really do like meatballs. A lot." She still said nothing, but her eyes moved to the next person's plate.

"Please." I smiled and held my plate within her reach for one more moment before I got to the sauce.

"Only 'cause you said please, and don't be telling anyone else that I gave you extra meatballs."

At the end of the table, I grabbed bread, a white foam cup of tea, and a napkin. The people in front of me had already sat down, so I couldn't act like I was part of their group. I glanced around searching for somewhere to sit. In the kitchen, in front of the stove was Tony stirring the sauce. Tony from Naples. I couldn't believe it.

I balanced my food, tea, bread, and plate in one hand and waved at him. He looked surprised, smiled, and waved back. With my eyes still on Tony's smile, my shirt became cold and wet. I looked down just in time to watch my spaghetti and meatballs slide right off the paper plate and unto the floor. Tea ran down my legs.

I bent down to clean up the mess and reached for the pile of napkins at the end of the table. My hand knocked over the basket full of the plastic utensils. All the white plastic forks, spoons, and knives fell into the heap of spaghetti. One fork landed straight up, like it was ready for someone to take a bite. I stood and placed the basket back on the table. And when I came back to the mess, Tony's fuzzy arms were there with a dish rag and a bucket.

"Didn't you like my spaghetti?" Tony said and made a playful mad face. His eyebrows came together like a wooly caterpillar. Our heads bumped as he picked up a handful of the plastic and noodles and threw it into his bucket. I used the napkins to wipe the tea from the floor. The corners of Tony's mouth turned upward and he said, "Lacy, you didn't have to throw it on the floor."

"I didn't mean to, I ... I," I said piling the napkins and some noodles on the plate.

Tony grinned and the smell of cigarettes and sweet tomatoes followed his words. "Go to the bathroom and get cleaned up. I'll take care of the rest. Go on."

As I stood up, more spaghetti noodles fell to the ground. I picked a couple of noodles off my legs and placed them on the napkin heap. My jean shorts were wet, and the dark blue circle made it look like I had peed on myself. When I walked to the bathroom, it seemed like everyone was staring at me. With the paper towels, I wiped my legs clean and soaked up some of the tea from my shorts. I wanted to run upstairs and change, but I couldn't do that. So I soaked up all that I could. If I walked fast and kept my back to the tables, I could get another plate of food and sit down without anyone noticing my stain. The other option was to leave, sneak back upstairs to my closet, and go without food, but I was too hungry for that.

I opened the bathroom door, and Tony was waiting for me.

"I thought you might need this," he said and handed me a Naples' apron.

"Thanks, I really do. It looks bad." I pointed to my stain.

"We've got some catching up to do. But first, my spaghetti. I fixed you another plate. Come on." Tony led me to the first table. One of the few families with small children was seated there; most of the people at the supper were gray-haired couples. Across from where Tony had put my plate sat a two- or three-year-old little boy with dark black curls and spaghetti all over his face. As I sat down, he grabbed a handful of saucy noodles and stuffed them in his mouth. Tony smiled and said, "You should feel right at home at this table, Lacy. I've got to finish making the desserts. We'll talk after I'm done, okay?"

"Yeah, thanks again for the apron," I said and took a bite of my garlic bread.

As I finished my meal, I noticed Tony at the door of the kitchen. He wiped his hand on his apron and gave me a quick wink. Rising from one of the tables, Annie from the AA meetings walked to the doorway of the kitchen and hugged Tony. I wondered how they knew each other. She talked and Tony nodded and smiled. Annie made a sweep with one of her arms over the roomful of people eating, and I guessed she was showing Tony how much everyone enjoyed his food. Pastor Kurt joined them. All their eyes lit on me. I knew they were talking about me because that weird feeling like you're naked, but you're not, circled around me. Annie, Tony, and Pastor Kurt deep into their conversation moved into the kitchen. I had to shake the feeling, so I went to the bathroom.

"Excuse me, what's your name?"

"Lacy," I said stepping out of the bathroom and holding the door for a woman. I recognized her. It was Bluebell—different clothes, same hair.

"Who are you here with tonight? Your parents? I'd love to meet them. Did you get enough to eat? I sure hope so. Don't worry about that spill earlier, we should've been using sturdier plates for spaghetti! Did your family just move here? I don't think I have seen you around, I would've remembered you."

Before I could speak, another woman came beside Bluebell. Both women stared at me. Their eyes kept going above my eyes to my hair.

"Peggy, did you meet Lacy? She's new here at the church. I

haven't met her parents, but .... Where do you get your hair done? I don't think I've seen *anybody* with a haircut quite like that before," Bluebell said, grabbing Peggy's arm and pulling her close.

"I cut my hair."

"Really? Well, I don't know why anyone would want their hair that short?" Bluebell looked at Peggy.

"I bet it's cool in this hot weather," Peggy said.

Bluebell pulled on Peggy's arm again and said, "Where did you say you were from?"

I wanted to get away from these women. They weren't going to rest until they met my parents, found out where I lived, and lectured me on the reasons why I shouldn't cut my own hair.

"I see you've met my niece, Lacy," a deep voice said behind me. When Annie reached me, she placed her arm around my shoulder and squeezed. She grinned at Bluebell.

"Your niece, I didn't know—"

"My sister's daughter, from up north. And actually, up north this hairdo is in style. What do they call it Lacy? I think you said it's ... the *punk* look. You know, Myrtle, I was thinking about getting my hair cut just like this." Annie touched the tips of my porcupine hair.

"Annie, I didn't know you had a sister."

"Oh yeah, I do, we just don't talk about her much. She's the black sheep of the family, living up north and all," Annie said and led me up the stairs. "Bye, ladies. Hey, isn't it nice that you all didn't have to cook this year? You go relax and enjoy the rest of the supper," Annie said over her shoulder as we reached the main level.

Annie walked into the sanctuary and I followed. She flipped on the lights, and I sat down on the last bench.

"Comfort makes cowards. You know what I mean, Lacy?" Annie motioned for me to slide over so she could sit down.

"No, I don't know what you mean," I said and wondered why she had claimed me as her niece.

"When people are comfortable with the things around them, it's hard for them to accept anything different. It upsets them. Sometimes they lash out or, in Myrtle's case, they're downright rude. Tony told me a little bit about you. I hope you don't mind," she said. Annie stared at me and waited for an answer. She looked so long that I noticed the yellow flecks that dotted her hazel eyes.

"No, I don't mind." I said, breaking my eyes away. My fingers rubbed the top of the bench ahead of me. I liked the smooth wood. Knowing she wasn't serious, I teased, "I could cut your hair for you, if you want?"

"Maybe sometime. I don't know if Myrtle could stand it. It's tempting, could you imagine the look on her face if I came to church with that hairdo? Oh!" Annie slapped her knee and laughed. "I could get me a leather vest and wear that too!" Annie was silent and stared for a moment, she must have been living the scene in her head because she snickered before she spoke again. "No ... I really like my ponytail. If I had spiky hair like that, I'd try to blow dry it or put gel in it, I wouldn't be able to leave it alone. Too much work for me fussing over hair. Speaking of work," Annie said, shifting to sit up taller. "I have a deal for you. Interested?"

"I don't know, the last deal I had wasn't a very good one."

"This is good. It'll work for both of us. I have a farm. A berry farm. Blueberries, strawberries, blackberries. It is a lot of work." She made picking motions with her hands. It seemed like Annie used gestures for almost every word. If I were her hands, I'd be tired. "Anyway,"—she rubbed her palms together—"the blueberries are almost ready. I really could use the help. It's a self-pick farm, but I need someone to check customers out while I'm helping the others get started on picking. You help me with my farm, and I'll help you find your real dad in Reidsville."

"I don't know, I'll—"

"Lacy, Tony and I are good friends. I know you don't have anyone right now to help you. Before you answer, I've got to tell you something that may have an impact on your decision. Pastor Kurt knows you're living here at the church. I guess he found your things in a closet. He's ready to call in the professionals to assist you."

I slid myself down and out the other end of the bench. As I walked toward the door behind Annie, she reached for my arm.

"Wait, hear me out. Please." It was the kindness in her *please* that stopped me.

"Pastor Kurt's a great guy, but he's got to call someone about you. It's his job. Now, I have talked to him on your behalf. I hope you don't mind." She touched her chest and looked at me. When I didn't answer or look her way, she continued, "I'm not going to ask you why you ran away—that's your business. Pastor Kurt is willing to let you stay with me and not call anyone. I told him I'd take care of everything. It's hard work at the farm, but my neighbor, he has some connections. I know he could help locate your father. The way I see it, you have a couple options. You could leave here right now and be on the run again with no one to help you, or you could come to the farm with me. The decision is yours." Annie let go of my arm.

I walked to the doorway of the sanctuary and stopped. After a month at the church, I still had no plan, no way of getting to Tommy Franco. I thought about Boots and Flo and knew there must be others like them. I was afraid of running, but I was afraid to trust Annie even more.

"Listen, you'd be doing me a favor by staying at my place and helping me through the summer. Please."

"Okay," I heard myself say. It was as if the word just slipped out. I would help her—but I didn't have to trust her—*and* I'd make sure that she did what she promised. I walked back to her. "I'll help you with your berries, and you'll help me find my father. I don't know anything about berries, but if you tell me what to do, I'll do it. I want to get to my father, so I'll work hard. If you don't do what you say, I'm leaving."

I stood behind Annie. "And, don't try to give me to anybody, I work for you and you work for me." Annie stood and turned her body to face mine.

"Well—" Annie started.

I remembered something else to add to the deal, so I spoke over her. "And one more thing, I want transportation to Reidsville." I held my hand out so we could officially shake on the deal.

Annie's forehead smoothed and her cheeks plumped as she smiled. She leaned one knee on the bench and grabbed my hand, squeezing it firm.

"You drive a hard bargain, Lacy. It's a deal, transportation and all. And just so you know, Annie Dawson Smith always keeps her word."

~

I got your second letter today. Did you ever go to see him? I went once. It was after my fifteenth birthday.

You have nice handwriting, actually your lettering reminds me of my mother's. The last few weeks, Annie and I planted lots of vegetables. We have a small garden off to the side of the house—we don't sell those veggies, we eat them.

Last Sunday, the pastor's sermon was about forgiveness. I thought about me, I thought about you, and I thought about him.

From what I can tell, it's a lot easier to talk about forgiveness than to actually do it. Annie, says that time heals. I don't know if I believe her, I think it takes more than time. I hope that one day you can forgive me.

Lacy

10

A ll of June and July of that summer, I learned a lot about blueberries. Like, fire ants are good to have in the blueberry rows. I hate fire ants, but so do cutworms, leaf rollers, and maggots. And those insects can ruin a crop. When I came to the farm, we had to inspect the bushes for yellow-necked caterpillars every week. We never found any, but Annie warned me about them too many times to count. "It's like a caterpillar convention, they can wipe out a bush in no time," she'd say on our Monday morning walks through the rows. All her bushes were in the family of rabbiteye, which I thought was a funny name. But when I looked at the blueberries, they really did look like the eyes of a rabbit. Annie's farm had two kinds of bushes: Becky blue, which had berries early and powder blue, which had berries midsummer. The Becky blues were my favorite.

I kept my end of our deal. Every day, I sat in the three-sided wooden shed with the scale and the cash box. I weighed the customer's berries, took their money, and tried to sell them elephant garlic. Annie told me she'd pay me a quarter for each one I sold.

And she kept her word and helped me with my search. She had me write a letter to Tommy Franco explaining who I was and that I wanted to meet him. I didn't tell her how I knew that Tommy was my father; it's hard to explain something you feel. And I didn't show her the letter Tommy wrote my mother, maybe it was because he called himself an asshole—I was afraid that Annie wouldn't help me find someone like that. I knew Tommy Franco wasn't an asshole, he came back for me and he loved my mother. She lied to me and she lied to Tommy. All Annie needed to know was that Tommy Franco was my real father and Samuel Mitchell was my stepfather.

I showed her the newspaper clipping and the black-and-white photo, and she asked me a lot of questions. She said the information was needed to find Tommy. When Mr. Williamson, Annie's neighbor and a retired police detective, found four possible matches, I copied the letter three times and we mailed them to all the Francos. It's funny, I never thought that Tommy Franco would've moved from Reidsville. But not one of the four possible matches lived in Reidsville—the closest one was in Moyock, North Carolina.

The first time I met Mr. Williamson, he bragged about his connections with the police in Durham and his abilities to find people. I was glad he could *find people*, but I was worried he'd turn me in. Annie must have seen the concern on my face because later that night she told me that Roger Williamson was harmless, he wasn't going to call anyone to come get me. She'd known him for years, she said, and he wouldn't go against her wishes. I kept my duffel bag packed for the first two weeks. Just in case.

"How about some excitement tonight?" Annie said as she handed me a washed plate to dry.

"Excitement?" I had been with Annie for a while and we hadn't really left the farm. I rubbed the plate with the green-

and-white plaid towel and waited to hear what kind of excitement she had planned before I said yes.

"The Fireman's Fair!"

"What is the Fireman's Fair?"

"It's a carnival that comes to town every summer and all the
proceeds from the fair go to help buy the volunteer firemen the
equipment they need." She handed me a glass. Her wet fingers
slipped, and the glass fell right into my towel. "It's fun, games,
cotton candy, rides. Come on, I know *all* the best rides. *And* Mr.
Williamson works the Ferris wheel, he'll let us ride over and
over for free!"

GREEN, red, blue, and white lights hung from strands and
outlined the tops of the rides. At the entrance, The Fair was
written on a sign with a moving light that traced the sign's
rectangular borders. As we walked through the entrance, I
watched the light switch from one bulb to the next. We melted
into the crowd. The machines that powered the rides hummed
so loud that bits of people's conversations swirled around in the
air, pink candy clouds floated by me on white paper cones,
screams and laughs shot out from the rides, and French fries
overflowed from giant red-and-white striped buckets and dotted
the ground. It was magic.

I wished I lived at the Fireman's Fair. Maybe, I thought, I
could put rides together or sell cotton candy. It had to be fun
watching people enjoy themselves. And then, I'd pack up, move
to the next town and watch *those* people have fun, never ever
losing the feeling myself.

"Momma," a little blond boy with a striped shirt yelled. He
ran four or five steps and stopped with his arms out for balance.
His body swayed from front to back and side to side. When his
body centered, he ran another few steps. I followed his gaze and

saw his mother on one knee holding out her arms for him. When the boy reached his mother, she wrapped her arms around him, and spun in a circle.

"Did you and Daddy enjoy the ride?" she said and kissed his neck until he giggled. When she placed him back on the ground, the boy grabbed her legs and then lifted his arms up toward the mother again and grunted. The mother bent over and kissed his forehead and said, "You're a big boy, you can walk."

Why didn't my parents love me like that? My feet dragged across the pavement. I wondered what my mother was doing right now. I was sure they'd gone to the liquor store that afternoon, and I was sure they were already drunk. Why hadn't we ever had fun together? And why had everything revolved around their bottles? I kicked at the wrappers, the French fries, and the cotton candy cones. Annie had walked a few feet ahead of me, but she glanced back when a piece of trash I kicked hit her heel. I said sorry and then turned for one more look at the boy.

He now held both of his parents' hands. Together, they swung the boy's body forward and he laughed. A picture of Samuel Mitchell dragging my mother down our hallway flashed in my mind. I felt like thirty people stood on my shoulders. I'm not sure what I tripped on, probably my own feet. In the swarm of happy people, I curled up on my side and wished that the pavement would open and swallow me. But it didn't. The light strands that connected the rides were hazy, and against the black sky, the bulbs seemed to shine brighter than before. I wiped under my eyes with my shirt. Annie put her hand down, helped me to my feet, and never said a word.

I brushed the bits of pavement off my palms and looked around again. Yeah, the fair *seemed* magical at night, but in the daylight, it would look like heaps of metal and trash. Fireflies were like that too. When I was little, I'd catch them, put them in a glass jar and name them as I fell asleep. The fireflies told me their stories and gave me a light show. Light without heat—a magical secret I learned later. In the morning, my jar was full of silent brownish-gray beetles with no flashing tails. The magic was gone, so I'd open the metal-punctured top and let them go.

"Step over here, ladies, and be a queen," a teenage boy peppered with pimples said into his bullhorn.

"Let's go, Lacy. I love these games. I'm not any good, but it's fun." Annie grabbed my arm and led me over to the booth. The sign over our head read, The Queen's Crown. Light bulbs formed the letters, and the word *crown* was a combination of blue, green, and red bulbs.

"Now, my fair ladies, it's really easy to get yourself a crown." He'd put the bullhorn down and held in his hand three rings. "If you can get the ruby"—he flashed the red ring—"the emerald, and the sapphire on the queen's crown, you win your own crown." The boy placed the green ring, the red ring, and the blue ring on the necks of three gold spray-painted glass bottles. Set in holes in a wooden block, the bottles looked like a crown. The center bottle was the highest and the other two bottles were equal in height.

"Which one of you lovely ladies would like to try to win this!" he said holding up a plastic tiara.

"Me," Annie said and stepped forward. "I've always wanted to win this game. They have it every year, and for the life of me, I can never win."

"I'll watch."

"No, I want you to play. Please." Annie wrapped her arm around my shoulders.

"Here you go, little lady. The jewels for the queen's crown," the boy said as he handed me the rings with one hand and took Annie's dollar with the other.

I pitched my rings. They went nowhere near the bottles, and I didn't care. Annie took the rings and paid the boy another dollar. He called out to others walking by, "Come see this lady try to win a crown." Her first ring almost hit the boy in the head. The second, the sapphire, landed on the ground in front of the bottles. And the third ring, the ruby, looped around the center bottle. Annie jumped up and down.

"I have to play one more time, Lacy. I've never gotten one ring on before."

The boy took her money and handed her the jewels again. An old woman and a little girl came over to watch. Annie threw the blue ring, it caught the neck of one of the side bottles, spun around, and rested. Annie jumped and grabbed my arm. She aimed the green ring for the other bottle on the side. A flake of gold paint came off the bottle as the emerald clanked around the neck.

"Oh my, you throw the last one, Lacy. I can't."

Annie handed me the red ring. I didn't want to, I told myself. I would lose the crown and all the luck that Annie had. But somewhere deep inside, I wanted to throw the ring, I wanted it to loop around the center bottle and I wanted my life to be magical. "It's impossible," I heard myself say. I stared at the center bottle.

"Throw it," the little girl said and leaned against the booth.

The red ring left my fingers.

I felt the heaviness come again when I watched the ruby land on the ground, nowhere near the bottles. I had ruined everything.

"Give her another chance," the old woman said to the boy.

"Well, I'm really not supposed to—"

"You have to do what my grandma says, or she'll get a switch," the little girl said.

"Don't make me get a switch after you, boy," the old woman said and playfully shook her finger at the boy and smiled at me.

He placed the red ring on the wooden counter in front of me.

I couldn't touch it. The girl tugged at the bottom of my shirt and said, "I know a secret."

I looked down into her face. Her chubby finger told me to come closer. I leaned down, and she whispered in my ear, "You can do it. You have to be like the little red train and think you can. That's what my mommy always says."

I picked up the ruby ring. The ring burned like fire in my hand. I thought about Boots and how he burned me. I thought about Samuel Mitchell and how he beat me. I thought about my mother and how she lied to me. Tears flooded my eyes, and I flicked the ring.

Annie jumped, the little girl clapped, and her grandmother said, "The second time's the charm, sweetie." I wiped my eyes and saw the ruby ring resting on the center bottle's neck.

"Who gets the crown?" the boy asked Annie as he pulled a plastic tiara off the shelf above our heads.

"We'll share it! She'll get to wear it when she stops feeling sorry for herself." Annie looked in my direction and slipped the crown on her head.

"You look like a real queen," the girl said to Annie as they walked away.

ANNIE and I strolled through the crowd. Some people looked at Annie's crown and shook their heads. Almost all the little girls told their parents that they wanted a crown too. Annie stood taller with her crown and waved to the Fireman's Fair kingdom. When I looked over at her, she squeezed her lips together, twisted her mouth, and crossed her eyes. I tried not to smile and told her that her eyes would stay like that if she didn't stop. She laughed and said it was worth the risk. By the time we reached the Ferris wheel, Annie had perfected her royal wave, and my fingertips were pink and sticky from the cotton candy that she *had* to buy for me.

"My, my, my, it's the queen and her lady-in-waiting," Mr. Williamson said. Annie did a curtsy. "Did you steal that crown?"

"Why, Roger!" Annie pitched her voice up high and spoke like someone from England. "I won it fair and square. Well, actually, my lady-in-waiting and I won it together."

"Very good then, your majesty. Would you like a ride?" he pointed to the back of the line. "No cutting, even for the queen." He winked at us.

The line moved quickly. Annie was the first in our car. She wiggled back and forth and the car rocked. I stepped in and held the bar as Mr. Williamson dropped a metal pin through a hole, locking us in. My fingers traveled up to my shoulders hunting for a piece of hair to twist. Nothing. So they wrapped themselves around the black metal bar in front of me. I slid my cupped hands along metal, stopping on two spots where the paint had been worn away to a dull sticky black. Who else had gripped this bar? The fact that other people had rubbed a place for my hands made me feel better about being scared, but not about the ride.

I'd never ridden a Ferris wheel before, but I wasn't going to let Annie know that. When I was eleven, we'd gone to a carnival, though it was nothing like the Fireman's Fair. It had less than ten rides and they only sold popcorn. Samuel wouldn't let me on any of the rides. My mother tried to convince him that the rides were safe and to let me ride just one other than the carousel. But because he was a welder, he knew about joints and machinery, and he never trusted the workers that put the rides together.

The wheel moved, rocking our car, and my fingers gripped tighter around the metal bar. Mr. Williamson let riders off and locked the new riders in. It seemed to take forever before the wheel started to turn.

"Are you having fun?" Annie asked as our car climbed backward toward the top.

I nodded yes and peeked over the side of the car. The wind brushed against my neck, and I looked at the people waiting for their turn. Some waved their hands in the air and smiled, others looked ahead to the entrance of the ride, and some had formed clusters with people facing each other and not paying attention to the gaps in the line. As we reached the top again, their faces blurred, and they looked like toys.

I closed my eyes and imagined I was a butterfly—a monarch. Orange-and-black wings extended out of my sides, and I soared.

The wheel jerked, and I opened my eyes. Mr. Williamson stopped at the car right in front of ours, unlocked the bar and helped the people out. I realized that we were going to be the last to leave the ride.

"Monarch butterflies are one of the longest living butterflies," I said as the wheel turned backward and the car climbed.

"Really, how long do they live?"

"If they have to migrate, about eight months."

"Wow, that's longer than I thought. Don't most butterflies live only a few weeks?" Annie said. With a loud screech of metal, our car stopped again, and Mr. Williamson switched the riders with the waiters.

"Some types can live for a couple of months."

"The way caterpillars eat I would think that the butterflies would live longer!" Annie laughed. Our car moved to the top of the wheel, and with our backs to the fair, we both looked out into the night sky.

"I bet people would live differently if we only had eight months to live," Annie said into the air. She looked at me and said, "I knew you were there that day."

"What?"

"At that first AA meeting, I knew you were there, sitting on the stairs. I knew I'd meet you, and I knew that we would help each other."

I stared into the darkness. Annie filled the quiet. "Lacy, was there any other reason that you left home? Besides finding Tommy? No pressure, you don't have to tell me, but I'm here if you want to talk."

I'd known it would be just a matter of time before she would ask me why I ran away. Even though she'd promised no questions, she was too nice of a person not to ask. A black flake of paint clung to the bar. I worked my fingernail under the edge and scratched the bar, working the flake free. Underneath the paint, the silver metal was exposed. She would keep asking until I told her something. So, I decided a quick answer that said it all would be best.

"My stepfather hit me, and I just got tired of it."

Annie nodded. For a few moments, she seemed far away. I thought that we were done talking, but she spoke again. "Did your parents drink?"

"Yeah."

"Alcohol changes people. Don't get me wrong, it's terrible to hit anyone, but sometimes people don't know what to do with the pain in their lives. From my experience ... the pain has to go somewhere. It either stays inside or you take it out on other people."

"Did you know that fuzzy caterpillars turn into moths and slick caterpillars turn into butterflies?"

Annie didn't have time to answer because it was our turn to get off the Ferris wheel. Mr. Williamson unlocked the bar. I got out, and Mr. Williamson held out his hand for Annie and placed his other hand on her lower back. He hadn't helped anyone else exit the ride the way he helped Annie. I smiled. He must have noticed me staring and smiling because his face reddened.

"Another go on the wheel?" Annie asked when we exited the ride's ramp.

"Nope."

"Annie," Mr. Williamson called. He ran over with the plastic crown. "Here, you almost forgot! Your crown, Queen Annie." He handed the crown to Annie, and she put it on my head.

"I think it's Lacy's turn to be queen. Thanks, Roger."

He waved and ran back to the ride's controls. We walked through the fair. Most of the little children were gone, and teenagers had replaced them. I was ready to go back to Annie's.

"Can we go home?"

"Did you have a good time?"

"Yeah, it was a lot of fun. Thanks for bringing me here, I'm just tired."

"Are you feeling better than before we came?"

I nodded a yes and felt the crown move on my head. Annie reached up and adjusted it. She put her arm around my shoulder as we walked.

"We adults make mistakes. Big ones sometimes. But I'm sure, in time, you'll come to understand the why. The hard part is letting go of the hurt."

I DIDN'T UNDERSTAND what Annie was trying to tell me that night. Now I understand, but I'm still working on the letting go part. When I look back on that year, there isn't one experience I'd change because I learned so much. But if I had a chance to go back, I would change how I reacted to what happened after the berry season.

I t was August, a few weeks before my fourteenth birthday; I walked along the dirt rows through the blueberry bushes. No return replies had come from my letters. During the days, I kept busy in the field, helping customers or helping Annie, but at night, thoughts of Tommy Franco kept my mind busy. Annie got tired of me wondering out loud about him, told me to be patient, gave me the book *A Tree Grows in Brooklyn,* and said, "You'll like getting to know Francie." But *getting to know her* meant reading over three hundred pages. Annie read all the time. I had never read a book so thick; the ones I checked out of the school library were mostly paperbacks on different kinds of insects. We made a compromise. On the even days, I read about Francie and on the odd days, I read the pests sections of her gardening books.

I brushed my fingers against the bushes as I walked to the far side of the field. The berries were nearly gone. I ate a few of the ripe ones I found, but I had to work for them. Everyone had picked the outside of the bushes clean—the berries left were the ones deep inside. A tent of netting covered most of the bushes. In each corner of the field, tall poles held corners of the net, and in the middle rows, poles were randomly placed to support the center of the net. The netting didn't provide any shade, it was purely to keep the birds from eating all the berries. Annie had left a few rows of bushes uncovered. Freebies for the birds, she'd said. Because the season was almost over, the netting would come down soon.

The sun rose higher and the birds chattered to each other. Down at the far end of the field, a high-pitched cry interrupted my thinking. I followed the sound. Before I reached the knot in the net, I knew it was a trapped bird. There had been about eight birds tangled in the netting since I had arrived at Annie's. But Annie had always been the one to untangle them, and only once had she actually needed to cut the net. When I wasn't working at the shed, I'd watched how Annie freed the birds. So, I decided I would free this one.

I stepped to the outside of the rows of bushes. The bird was trapped at one of the lowest places in the net. As I neared the noisy black bird, its wings flapped and bits of sunlight shimmered on the feathers as they beat against the net. I didn't want to hurt the bird, but I didn't want to get my hand pecked either. I touched its tail feather, and the bird cried a loud screech and flapped its wings harder and faster, trying to fly away. I took a deep breath and remembered how Annie had freed the others. I cupped both hands around the bird starting from the head and I slowly let my hands close around its body. I shifted the bird so that I held it with one hand and untangled the twisted net from its feet with my other hand.

As I held the freed bird, it seemed light, lighter than I thought it would be. The yellow rim around its eyes was beautiful. I stroked its head; the feathers were slick. It was so peaceful now resting in my hand. I whispered goodbye, aimed the bird toward the sky, and released.

"Lacy, Lacy," Annie called from the back door of the house.

Annie's house wasn't at all like a farm house. Her house with red brick, black shutters, a flat wooden eagle perched over the top of the front door looked like it belonged in a subdivision. But when you stepped out from the garage, walked across the blacktop drive, and surrounded yourself with the berries, it was like crossing miles of land.

Annie was like her house. She seemed too polished to be a farmer. I always imagined farmers wearing overalls and talking with a piece of hay resting on their bottom lip. Annie didn't wear overalls; she wore jeans, T-shirts, and a wide-brimmed straw hat with a chin strap. And she never talked with anything in her mouth.

Annie yelled again, cupping her hands around her mouth. "Lacy! I need to talk to you, come on in the house."

When I got close enough to see Annie's face, I knew something was wrong. All the happiness of the last few months drained out of me.

"What's wrong?" I said.

She turned her head and looked inside the house, avoiding my face. She held the door open for me. "I need you to sit down and listen."

I stepped into the kitchen. My eyes had to adjust to the lack of bright sunlight and the cool air surrounded me. I pulled out a chair, sat, and waited. Annie followed behind me and kept going past the kitchen into the dining room. From the hutch, she pulled out some papers and came back to the table.

"When you first came here, Lacy, I ... I contacted your mother."

Annie smoothed a stack of handwritten papers. I said nothing. Heat came to my cheeks. Annie had betrayed me.

"I knew you were running from a situation that was bad. But if I had a daughter and she was gone and I didn't know where she was ... I would be insane with worry. So with Mr.

Williamson's help, I got your mother's phone number. And I called her. Lacy, when I told her you were all right and with me, she cried."

My mother cried. She always cried when Samuel hit her, but this time I'd been the one who caused her pain. I looked down at my hands.

"Your mother was so glad you were okay and safe. We talked for only a few moments the first time."

The first time. How many times had she talked to her? I studied Annie's face. I know why she looked so serious—he found out where I am, and he's coming for me.

"I called again. She told me a little bit about why she thought you left. And Lacy, she said she didn't blame you for leaving. She told me she wasn't much for talking on the phone. She asked me to take care of you. I told her that I would. She asked for a way to get in touch with me if she needed to. I didn't want to let you down and break your trust, so I gave her my brother's work address in Michigan. I told her to mail any letters there and he would mail them to me. She said that was fine, she knew you were safe but she still didn't know where you were. Each time, our phone conversations were short because she didn't want to be overheard. I did call one other time and a man answered the phone, so I hung up and never called again." Annie looked at me. "Are you okay?"

I didn't know what to think.

"A few weeks after the last phone call, I received a letter from your mother. I think you should read it." Annie said and handed me a three-page letter. My eyes skimmed the paper and I saw her *a*'s. I put the letter down and looked away. I didn't want to read it. I guess it was because the letter was something of hers, something familiar, or maybe I sensed Annie's fear as she handed me the letter.

"It's important, Lacy. Read it," Annie whispered.

. . .

DEAR ANNIE,

Please don't call anymore. I haven't been feeling very good lately. So my husband answers the phone. I stay in the bed most days. If I have any energy, I go into the back yard and sit on the grass. I have always loved the smell of fresh cut grass.

Some days, I remember when I was a little girl with my mother and father. Other times, I remember Lacy as a baby playing out in the backyard. She was a sweet baby. She would giggle and smile all the time, but I always thought her brown eyes looked way too big and deep for such a little face.

I miss her. I get sad thinking about the way my life worked out. But Lacy is one thing that was right. I wasn't a good mother. I couldn't keep her safe. I tried.

But Samuel ... I don't want you to think that my husband is a monster. He just can't control himself when he gets angry. He wasn't always like the way he is now. I made him that way.

Have you ever felt like second best?

I tried to keep it hidden inside me, but it didn't work. Now I know that whatever's inside you shows up on the outside in some way. Either in your eyes, by what you do, what you say, and sometimes the most hurtful of all, what you don't say. I never loved him the way he loved me. I think that kind of thing eats away at a man. It changed him.

I don't know why I'm telling you these things. Ever since you called me, I felt I could trust you. Lacy is better off with you than here right now. It's a hard time. I'm sick and Samuel doesn't know what to do, so he's angry all the time. He can't fix me. And he can't fix the things that have happened. I'm sure that he's sorry for everything. But I'm not sure if he would ever admit it.

Thanks for taking care of my baby. Protect her.

Justine

．　．　．

I LOOKED up from the letter and Annie stared at my face. She waited. I read the last few lines again. I didn't understand. Take care of me, protect me? Didn't she think I could take care of myself? Didn't she want me?

"I think you should read the letter that came yesterday in the mail. And then we will talk about what you want to do," Annie said and handed me the last paper under her hands.

DEAR ANNIE,

I hope you get this letter soon. I've gotten worse. I went to a doctor about a year and a half ago. He told me what I had and I didn't want to believe him. Even now, I can't write the word down. Early on, before Lacy left, I thought if I closed the idea out of my mind, I wouldn't be sick anymore. I knew I couldn't leave her alone with Samuel. So, I told no one and didn't get help when I should have.

I know you're thinking that I was stupid for denying the truth. And you're right. Having so much time to think, I know now that the truth should always be faced head-on.

My neighbor, Liz, is so good to me. She comes over when Samuel leaves and takes care of me. Liz is the one who has mailed the letters for me. I couldn't risk putting them in our mailbox.

Today she's taking me to the hospital. I don't want to go, but she says she's dragging me. I know they won't be able to do much for me, but maybe they can prolong it just a bit. I was hoping that I could see Lacy. Will you ask her to come home and see me? I'll understand if she doesn't come. But if she decides to come, will you please come with her?

Help her and please keep her safe.
Justine

．　．　．

I HELD the letters in my hands and squeezed. When I looked down, the letters were a ball of paper in front of me. Was she dying?

Her letters seemed like a different person than the one I knew. Going to see her meant I would have to see him. I couldn't go.

"Lacy, do you understand that your mother is very sick?"

"I'm confused .... Is she going to die?" I said.

"I don't know. I know you're afraid. I would be too if I were in your shoes." Annie took the paper ball and unfolded the letters. She ironed them with her hands over and over. "Sometimes you have to push through your fears."

A lot of advice Annie gave that summer seemed hard for me to understand—like math. I knew when she'd said something she wanted me to think deeply about because her head tilted to one side and she stared through me. At the moment she spoke, I kind of got the meaning of what she was telling me, but then it was gone. Just like when the teacher explained a math problem on the board and for a second after, I got it. But when I tried to do a problem on my own, it's gone.

"I don't know what to do."

"Your mother loves you, Lacy. If you want to go, I'll be with you all the time. Trust me, I've learned that fears are temporary but regrets last a lifetime." Annie laid her hands on top of mine.

I pulled away from Annie and left the kitchen table. I wasn't ready. I couldn't go back. It was strange, the thought of not seeing my mother ever again made me miss her. I couldn't explain it, and I didn't want to feel it. This time, I understood Annie's words. Not everything, but enough to know that I had to see my mother.

12

———

When I came out of my room, Annie had already packed a suitcase and put together a bag of snacks for the trip. Before we left that afternoon, she called Mr. Williamson and told him we were leaving and asked him to look after things. From Annie's short conversation with him, I guessed he already knew we were going.

The first part of the drive, we didn't talk much. Annie had a collection of tapes thrown into a basket between the seats of the van—she called out the name of the group she wanted to hear, and I fished out the tape.

A song about a spinning wheel and a painted pony played. It made no sense to me. I stared at the cassette cover and tried to figure out the song and the group's name. Blood, Sweat & Tears.

"Annie, why would this group name themselves after something gross, smelly, and sad?"

She laughed. "Maybe you've missed another meaning of their name."

The song finished and I still couldn't understand what it was about and had no idea what the group's name could've meant.

"I think you're really brave, Lacy. It takes a lot of courage to go back."

Brave? The last time we'd stopped for Annie to go pee, I looked for a trucker to catch a ride with. I didn't know where I'd go, but that didn't matter. The only thing that stopped me was that there were no trucks. I wasn't brave.

Annie was a good person and I appreciated her helping me, but good people don't understand bad people. She didn't know what we were going into, what I'd left.

"I think about my mom sometimes, but I don't miss being there."

Annie nodded and kept her eyes on the road.

"My real dad's going to make things right. I don't know why he didn't take me with him when I was four." I looped my index finger around the door lock and pulled it up and down, listening to the click.

"What do you mean?" Annie glanced at me.

"Tommy Franco came to see me when I was four, there was a big fight, Samuel and Tommy broke a table. After that, Tommy wrote my mom a letter. But I don't know why he didn't take me with him or come back again?"

"I wish I could tell you what he was thinking. Maybe he couldn't take you with him at that time."

"Did I tell you that he was a really good basketball player?"

"Yes, remember you showed me the clipping. Lacy, we'll find him and you can ask him your questions." Annie pointed to a tape case with children's faces in the middle of little flowers. I picked up the case and read the group's name: Peter, Paul and Mary. Good name, I thought.

The van filled with voices singing about a lemon tree, and Annie sang softly as she focused on the road. I was too tired to listen, so I rested my head against the window. The sun had dipped below the trees, and the tall grass and the roadside flowers whizzed by, making a steady stream of green. I closed my eyes and tried to imagine what my mother looked like in a hospital bed. I couldn't picture anything.

THE HALLWAYS WERE wide and smelled like cleaning spray. Except for the light-gray flecks in the tiles on the floor, everything was white. Morning sun flooded into the hospital. The brightness reminded me of being in snow.

After we gave the woman at the front desk my mother's name, she directed us by pointing her pen and spewing directions. I lost track of the twist and turns she had told us and so did Annie. We finally found the right elevator and pushed the number four.

The door opened. My heart pounded.

Room 434 was at the end of the hall past the nurses' station. Annie asked me if I was okay. I said yeah, but I was afraid. It had been five months since I had seen her. She probably hated me for running away and for leaving her alone with him.

She had been sick a long time, and I never knew. I thought back to the months before I left—her tired face, her daytime naps on the couch, her increased drinking.

I rested my back against the wall three doors away from her room. Annie left me and said she'd check to see if my mother was alone.

My mother had taken me to the hospital once. The neighbor's son, I can't even remember his name, had decided that we were going to ride the *big* hill. The plan: I'd drive and he'd *help* from the back. So, we wheeled his red tricycle up the hill. I got ready and held tight to the white rubber grips. He stepped onto the ribbed metal platform in back and with his foot, gave us an extra boost—for luck, he'd said. Halfway down the hill, my feet couldn't move at the speed of the pedals. Way too fast. I raised my feet and screamed. He jumped off the back and rolled, adding another boost of speed. The handle bars wobbled back and forth, and I lost control of those too.

I don't remember hitting the corner of the pickup truck's tailgate, but he told my mother that's what tore the gash in my chin. I do remember her holding me in her arms and running down a hospital hallway. She told me it had taken three nurses and her to hold me down so the doctor could sew me up. I'd cried for her to help me as the doctor's needle moved through my skin. And I remember she'd drawn shapes on the palm of my hand and asked me to guess what they were. The doctor tried to give me a plastic red car as a reward; I refused it. My mother picked me up, kissed my forehead, and offered me an ice cream cone. I'd buried my face in her neck and nodded yes.

Annie wrapped her arm around me and gently led me to the door of room 434. "I'm going to wait out here for you, Lacy. Don't be afraid. Your mom may not look like you remember, but she's still the same inside."

The woman in the bed was a large woman with short raven hair. I knew my mother hadn't changed that much. I looked past the bed and realized that behind a hanging curtain was another bed. I stepped in front of my mother's bed. The light from the window made this side of the room brighter. Her eyes were closed, and she looked lost in the bed. A clear tube ran from a hanging bottle to her arm. Her hair was matted underneath her head. Her skin looked like the covering around frogs' eggs, milky and see-through. I was afraid if I touched her, she'd slip away.

My eyes filled and I turned toward the window. I wiped the tears away with the bottom of my shirt and stared at the beige gravel that covered the roof of the hospital.

"Lacy?" a small voice said.

I looked at my mother. Her lips moved and she said my

name again—the voice *was* my mother's. I moved to the side of the bed. She lifted her hand, but she couldn't reach me. Her hand went back to the bed and I rubbed my fingertips across the top of her knuckles.

"You look beautiful. Your hair, I like it. It matches you," she said and smiled.

I reached up and combed what hair I could behind my ears. "What's this?" I said and pointed to the bottle that hung on the silver pole next to her bed.

"It's medicine that makes the pain not so bad. Please, Lacy, could you hold my hand? I want to make sure you're really here."

I slipped my hand underneath hers, but didn't close my fingers. She smiled and closed her eyes.

"I'm sorry, Mom."

"Shh, don't you be sorry." She opened her eyes and squeezed my hand. "I'm the one who should be sorry. Lacy, I love you. I know I may not have done the best job showing you that, but God knows I love you more than anything I have ever loved." Her eyes shut again and I noticed the dark half-moons that colored the space under her eyes. I watched my mother's weak smile, and I wondered if she was going to die.

"Lacy, there is so much I want to tell you. I was afraid I wouldn't get to see you again. Liz, my neighbor, she has something—something I've been working on since you left." She held my hand tighter, and I could tell she wanted to talk to me more, but was too tired. Her breaths were hard for her to take. I wanted to tell my mother about the time I had been away. About Butch, Flo, Annie, and blueberries. But she closed her eyes, and her grip on me loosened. I watched her chest rise and fall.

With my forehead against the glass of the window, my breath made a mist rug on the window. Tiny puffs of clouds dotted the blue sky. My mother seemed so small, even smaller than I remembered. She needed *me* to hold her hand now like she had done for me before.

"Lacy? Lacy?" my mother's voice squeaked.

"I'm right here." I went over and held her hand.

"Is Annie with you?"

"Yeah, do you want to meet her?"

"Yes."

I tried to pull away so I could go the door and get Annie, but my mother held tight. I was surprised by her strength in that moment. "I'm going to get Annie. I'll be right back."

Annie was just outside the door, leaning against the wall. She jumped when I popped my head out from the door frame. "She wants to meet you." Annie followed me and as we walked by the raven-haired woman, she moaned.

"Mom, this is Annie." Annie towered over the bed. Annie's hair was the same color as my mother's, but that's all that was the same. Annie's skin was rosy and alive, my mother's milky white skin was dying. When Annie stepped beside the bed and touched my mother's arm, I saw the difference between life and death.

"Lacy, could you wait out in the hall while I talk with Annie?"

I wanted to know what she was going to say. I should know, so I didn't move.

"Please," my mother's voice begged.

Annie glanced at me, her eyes saying, *Please.*

I walked out into the hallway.

13

"Annie, is my mom going to die before we can go back tomorrow?"

"No." She put her arm around me as we walked out of the hospital. "We need to do two things for your mother before we go back tomorrow. Can you get me from here to your neighborhood?"

WE HEADED TO MRS. ANDREWS' house to pick up whatever my mother had left for me. I'd always liked Mrs. Andrews—the fact that she had helped my mother while she was sick made me like her even more. In my neighborhood, everything seemed new but old at the same time. As we turned onto the street, the cement girl with wings still stood watch in front bushes of the corner house, all the same potholes were there, borders of black tar mixed with gravel trimmed the road, and most of the yards were carpets of dried, yellow grass.

The van crept up the hill. My street was like a cursive *m*, two hills on either end and a valley in the middle. Our house was in the center of the valley. The Andrews' house was diagonally across from us. I pointed to the white house with gray shutters and Annie turned the van into the skinny driveway.

Annie turned off the engine. "I'm glad your mother has had someone to care for her. Lacy, I want to be honest with you. I'm not sure how much time your mother has left, maybe days. So, if there is something you want to say to her, say it. Don't hold it in." Annie didn't wait for me to say anything in response. She made her way quickly to Mrs. Andrews' front door. My mother must have told Annie what was killing her. I didn't want to know what *it* was.

I got out and stood on Liz's grass, staring at the red brick box I used to live in. The house looked tired—the white paint had flaked off the metal twisted rails that trimmed our front porch, no hanging pots of flowers decorated the eaves, and the rose bush hung over the sidewalk leading to the porch, daring anyone to walk to the door.

"Come on, Lacy. I think Liz is expecting us."

MRS. ANDREWS TOLD us how she took care of my mother and how my father had lost his job two weeks ago. She didn't say it was because of his drinking, but I guessed that's why.

"I've got to go to work shortly. I'm sorry our visit can't be longer," Mrs. Andrews said and pulled a large manila envelope from under a stack of papers on her dining room table and placed it into my hands. "This is what your mother's been working on."

"Thank you for everything you've done for Justine," Annie said.

"I didn't do everything I could've." Mrs. Andrew went back into the dining room and came out with another envelope just like mine. "Annie, this is for you."

"Do you have a pen?" Annie said.

"On the counter." Mrs. Andrews pointed to the kitchen.

Annie walked into the kitchen, and Mrs. Andrews stared at me, her eyes filled with pity. I knew she was trying to find something to say, but what is there to say to a girl whose mother's dying.

I held the envelope in my hand and wondered what was inside. Mrs. Andrews watched as I peeled a corner of the flap open.

"Don't. Wait until you get to your hotel, honey," Mrs. Andrews said.

"Thanks again, I left what you needed on the counter. We have to go," Annie said, coming out from the kitchen empty-handed. Where was the envelope that Mrs. Andrews gave her? Annie shuffled me out the front door before I could ask her about the envelope.

With my hand on the van door, I looked again at my house. The square windows seemed so small. When I lived there, I never realized their smallness. Those windows were my gateways to the world. When I couldn't be outside, I'd stand on the couch and watch and imagine what I'd find when I could go out. I stared at the living room window, not sure of what I wanted to see. Samuel Mitchell was watching me. I didn't see the curtains move, I didn't see someone duck down, but I felt him. He knew I had come back.

When we got to the hotel room, Annie busied herself with some papers. I sat on the bed with my envelope beside me.

"I'm going to the front desk to make a couple of phone calls. I'll be back in a few minutes."

As the door closed behind Annie, I slid the worn pad of paper out of the envelope.

My mother's words started halfway down the page. I stretched out across the bed and began to read my mother's life.

. . .

DEAR LACY,

Where do I start? You've been gone three months and I miss you. I hope you remember some of the good things from living here. It wasn't all bad, was it?

Do you remember the story of where your name came from? I bet you've forgotten that story. I used to tell you it before bed when you were little.

SAMUEL and I had taken a drive one Sunday afternoon. I was swollen so big with you. It was July, and I only had one more month to go before my due date. But we were both restless that afternoon and driving in the country made Samuel feel good. We drove into the late afternoon, then we parked and walked down a trail to the river. I picked some tall white flowers on the way down to the water.

I looked at the flowers and noticed how the tiny blooms sitting together looked like lace. I thought that was so beautiful.

"Samuel, do you know the name of this flower?" I asked.

He looked back at me and said, "That's Queen Anne's lace and if you don't want chiggers, you'd better throw'em down."

"Chiggers?"

"Yeah, little black things that get under your skin and itch like hell."

I searched the flowers I held in my hand. No chiggers. These flowers were too beautiful to throw down. I brought the flowers to my nose. They didn't smell. These flowers were nature's lace, they didn't need to smell.

We reached the river bank and I plopped down on the small blanket that Samuel had spread out. "Samuel, if this baby's a girl I want to name her Lacy, after Queen Anne's lace."

"You want to name our kid after a weed?"

"No, a wild flower."

"It's a weed, Justine." Samuel pitched a small stone into the river. He looked for another stone and spoke again. "My mother told me a story about those *flowers*. There was this queen who was making lace, and she pricked her finger, and a drop of red blood fell into the center. Look, see the red dots."

The red center did look like drops of blood. But I was more interested in his mother. He never talked about his past. The only things that Samuel ever told me about his past were that his mother left his father when he was seven, and he left his father at fifteen. I asked him once why he left home, and he said that his father hated him.

"Did your mother tell you lots of stories?"

"Yeah, so many that I didn't know what was true or what she made up."

"What was her name?"

"She left us because we weren't exciting enough," Samuel said as he stood up. I knew that meant the end of the conversation—he was done. He stood with his back to me for a very long time. You moved inside me. I imagined you growing inside me, my own nature's lace.

"Lacy Marie Mitchell, what do you think about that for a girl? Lacy, of course, after Queen Anne's lace and Marie after my mother. And we'll have to think about a boy's name."

With his eyes still on the river, he said, "That's fine."

TODAY, I've been thinking about how strong you are, so much stronger than me.

I'm not doing good. I'm sick. I have to tell you things now that I'd hoped to tell you when you were a woman, but I know there isn't time. It seems I've always taken the easy way out all my life. Even as a child, you spoke your mind. I never told your father about the teachers' phone calls or about your sassiness in school. I figured that school must have been a place for you to let go and not face the kind of punishment you got at home.

I am sorry for what he's done to you. Your father has reasons for the way he acts. It's my fault. I changed him, Lacy.

I know you found some things of mine before you left. I noticed the shoeboxes in my closet were moved around. I guess you're wondering who Tommy is. He was someone very special in my life before I met Samuel.

The summer before my senior year in high school, Tommy and I started going steady (that's what we called being boyfriend and girlfriend back then). He was a senior too. On December 15, 1963, he gave me a promise ring and we were engaged. I know you think it's funny I remember dates. But when special things happen, I burn the date in my mind.

Our plan was to get married right after high school. I loved him, I loved everything about him. When his hair got wet, it curled in tight little rings against his neck, his smell—even now, I can close my eyes and smell him—and his smile, I couldn't think straight when he smiled at me.

We were very happy, and Tommy had a fantastic basketball season that year. I had never seen him play that good. Others noticed too and he won a scholarship to Duke. I think that's when his plans changed. I didn't know until much later that I was the only one in love.

After the season was over, he asked me if we could wait until he got settled in college and then get married. Our plan was to find a place during the summer after his freshman year at Duke. I'd work and keep us going while he finished his three years.

In April, my parents died and my mother's sister came to live with me in my parents' house so I could finish school. After I graduated, I had to go and live with my aunt in Hopewell. She was nice to take me in, but her and her husband fought all the time. He didn't want me there. My aunt was trying to help. I was a hardship and I knew it—but she never told me that. So, I looked forward to Tommy and I having our own place.

The summer after I graduated, I got a job at the Coleman Shoe Factory. I made shoes. Well, I didn't make the shoes, I checked the finished ones for mistakes. I saved my money, saved it for my wedding and saved it for the household I was going to set up. My aunt's husband demanded I pay rent. Which was fair, but it didn't leave me much money to save. I did what I could.

I wrote Tommy every weekend. At first, he wrote me, not every week, but maybe every two weeks. During the summer before he left for college, he'd call from his parents' house. He came to see me once that summer. Fourth of July. We went to the lake and watched the fireworks. If he was distant, I didn't notice. I was so excited to have him near me again, to hold his hand, to smell his skin, and to kiss him.

As the fall approached, his letters stopped coming. But I kept writing him. I told him all about the wedding plans. I even sent him a magazine picture of the bridal shoes. I'd saved for them and with my employee discount, they were a great buy.

Did I tell you that the factory had a store attached to the front side of the building? Oh, Lacy, the shoes were fantastic, great quality too. Maybe I'm biased because I had a hand in making them.

Being at college made it nearly impossible for Tommy to call. I missed him so much. So, you can only imagine how excited I was when I got a letter saying that he was coming to see me. I was on cloud nine. It was right before Thanksgiving, so I decided to make the weekend very special.

A few weeks before Tommy's letter, my aunt saw Tommy. She had gone to Reidsville regarding my parents' will. He was visiting his parents. I think it was his mother's birthday. When I asked my aunt how he looked and if he asked about me, she was short with her answers. Later, I found out why. But at that moment, I saw what I wanted to see and nothing else.

The weekend Tommy came to visit, I fixed an early Thanksgiving dinner. My aunt and uncle went away for the weekend. By the time Tommy got in that Saturday afternoon, everything was ready.

After we cleaned up, we sat on the couch in the living room chatting about nothing in particular. Tommy leaned in and kissed me. I had missed him so much, and I was so in love with him, I didn't think, my heart and body took over.

I had been waiting, waiting until we got married. Maybe I knew that I was losing him. Now it's easy to say that was the reason we made love—especially looking back. But the truth is, I'd wanted to give him everything.

The next morning, I made breakfast before Tommy had to head back home. I poured his coffee and thought about breakfast with him every day for a lifetime.

"Isn't this great," I said.

"Yeah, great eggs."

"No, Tommy, this. You and me having time together like this."

"Oh, this. Yeah, it's great too. Justine—"

"When we get married, it will be just like this all the time. Let's set the date." I turned off the burner and brought the bacon to the table. I watched his face as I spoke. "Why don't we get married next month? I don't need anything fancy. I have a dress picked out, and I have enough money saved to buy it."

He moved the scrambled eggs around his plate and then put his fork down and looked away. "I'm not ready for marriage, Justine."

"What? Tommy, we've been planning this all year."

"No, you've been planning."

I couldn't even eat. My stomach felt like it was riding in a quickly dropping elevator.

"This is not funny, quit joking around."

"I'm not kidding. I'm not ready to get married, and I promised myself I would tell you this weekend. I've been trying all weekend, but there never was a good time. I didn't want to ruin your meal and last night was, well, unexpected." He pushed his plate toward the center of the table and leaned back in his chair. "I came here this weekend to tell you I think we should see other people. Put things on hold, date other people to make sure we're the right ones for each other."

By this time, I knew he wasn't joking. Tears filled my eyes and I said, "Tommy, I don't want to see anyone else. I love you, and I know you are the one I want."

"I'm not that sure, Justine."

With tears streaming down my cheeks, I looked at Tommy's face and noticed he wasn't even upset. He sipped his coffee and brought his plate back in front of him. I stood up grabbed my plate and his, but not before he was able to snatch a piece of bacon off it. "Who is she?" I said.

"What did your aunt tell you?" Tommy said chewing on his bacon.

"What?"

"That girl I was with when I saw your aunt a few weeks ago was just a friend. I knew she'd blow it up into something it wasn't. I don't need this shit, Justine." He pushed back from the table, the chair legs screeching against the floor, and he stood facing me. "I want to be able to do what I want with who I want. I really care for you, but I feel like I have a noose around my neck and you keep pulling it tighter and tighter." Tommy poured his coffee down the sink. "I want my freedom. We can still see each other, but other people too. Do you understand?"

"I understand perfectly." I threw the dish rag into the sink. I left him in the kitchen and went back to my room and shut the door. Secretly, I hoped he would come back and comfort me, but he never did. I heard him moving around in the kitchen and then I heard the front door close. I cried until I fell asleep.

I CALLED in sick the first three days of the week and didn't even get out of bed. I finally went to work on Thursday. All day, I replayed the conversation with Tommy, wondering what I could've said that would've changed his mind. A couple of times I missed shoes with flaws. By the end of my shift, I was drained. So, when some of the girls asked me to go out with them after work, I said yes. I had never gone before, but I was a free woman now.

We ended up at a tiny bar that had a pool table, an old Wurlitzer jukebox, and a dance floor the size of a book of matches. The girls guessed that something had happened between Tommy and me, so I told them. While I babbled and cried about Tommy, they took turns buying me beers. By the third beer, my head was fuzzy, and that felt a lot better than thinking clearly. One of the girls put some money in the jukebox. "Rockin' Robin" came on, and the four of us got up and danced. We had to push some tables back so we could move our arms without hitting each other. The music was so happy, I moved to it and I let myself go. Each time I'd spin around, I noticed a guy staring at me from the bar. He didn't smile, but he just stared with his straight brown hair swept over one eye.

When the song was over, I went back to the table. The jukebox played a slow song, and I was about to sit down when someone tapped me on the shoulder.

"Wanna dance?"

I looked up, it was the guy from the bar. His voice was deep and he pushed his hair away from his chocolate brown eyes.

"Yes, I would."

I placed his hands on my lower back and I rested my hands on his shoulders. We began to sway to the music.

"What's your name?" he said.

"Justine. And yours?" His eyelashes were long and his hair kept falling over his eye.

"Samuel. But my friends call me Sam."

"Nice to meet you, Samuel."

"You were dancing hard earlier," he said and combed back his hair with his fingers. It was almost long enough to stay behind his ear, but not quite.

"Yeah, just having some fun." He stared at my face, like he was memorizing it. I looked away and hoped that he would stop. He didn't.

"You're beautiful," he said.

I could see in his eyes that he meant what he'd said. His friends watched us dance and yelled Samuel's name, and lifted their beers in congratulations.

"What's that all about?" I asked.

"They didn't believe I'd ask you to dance. And they didn't believe you'd say yes."

"Oh, really?" I lifted up my head and stretched to reach his lips. My plan was to kiss him lightly, just a peck, but he kissed back. His hands pressed into my back, pulling me closer. His friends clapped and whistled when he released me.

"Thanks for the dance, Justine," Samuel said as he walked me back to the table. He left and my girlfriends swarmed around me.

"What was that?" they all asked, laughing and handing me another beer. I just shook my head and smiled. I didn't answer because I didn't know what had just happened, but compared to what I had been saturated in since Tommy left on Sunday, this was a good feeling.

Every so often I would look over my shoulder to the bar. I knew he was still there, but I wanted to see his eyes. Each time I looked his way, he was staring at me. He never smiled. Tommy melted butter with his smile and he used this ability to get whatever he wanted. I liked Samuel's seriousness, it was honest.

Finally, someone played a slow song. The Righteous Brothers began and I watched my friends' expressions. When they began to grin, I knew Samuel was coming for me. He didn't ask for the dance, he put his open hand in front of me. I placed my hand inside his and watched his hand swallow mine. As we danced again, he held me tighter than before and it was the middle of the song before he spoke.

He leaned down to my ear and whispered, "I want to keep you forever."

I reached for his lips again and this time kissed him hard. His arms tightened around me and I could hardly breathe. It felt good to be wanted.

I went home with Samuel that night.

IT WAS mid-January when I got the pregnancy test results from the doctor. I knew when I had gotten pregnant, but I didn't know who was the father.

I decided to tell Tommy I was pregnant with his child. I wanted him to be the father. I loved him and I thought if he knew I was carrying his child, he would marry me and we could live my dream.

With the money I had saved for my wedding, I bought a bus ticket to Durham, a black dress, a red scarf, and some snappy red shoes with black bows on the heels. The shoes were designer and cost me almost as much as the bus ticket, but I wanted to look beautiful for one of the most important moments of my life. My breasts were full and tingly, and with you growing inside me, I felt more like a woman than I ever had. I played my movie of telling Tommy about you in my head over and over. Each time, Tommy was more loving. By the time the bus reached Durham, Tommy was down on his knees swearing his love and begging me to be his wife.

I stepped off the bus and the air was warm for a Saturday night in the middle of January. I took this as a good sign. I was also glad because all I had for a coat was the shawl my aunt had lent me. I hadn't spoken to Tommy since that Sunday in November. From his previous letters, I knew the spots where he and his friends would probably be on a Saturday night.

The third place I went to, I found him. I didn't go to him right away, I found a booth in the back of the grill and tucked myself away and watched him.

Tommy held her hand. And then he brushed her red hair off her shoulder and kissed her neck. He pulled back and smiled. They kissed long and deep, a kiss that should have been reserved for a woman and man in a relationship of meaning. Not a relationship of just two months.

I wanted to go over and shake Tommy and the redhead, but I went to the bathroom and threw up instead. I reapplied my lipstick and reminded myself why I was there. I was here to tell him I was carrying his child, and now I was here to get him back. You gave me the strength I needed.

I strolled over to the table where Tommy and the redhead were sitting with two other couples. I took off my shawl and scarf, looked the redhead in the eyes and said, "Hi, Tommy."

"Holy shit, Justine, what are you doing here?" Tommy said.

"I'm Gail, Tommy's girlfriend. And you are?"

I touched Tommy's forearm and ignored Gail's question. "I've got some news for you," I said and hoped that my voice didn't reveal how scared I was.

"Send a letter," Tommy said and pulled his arm away.

"Tommy, who is this?" Gail asked.

"This kind of news is something that has to be said in person." I glanced around the table at Gail and the others. "Do you want to talk here or can we go somewhere?" I was prepared to tell him in front of everyone, but I hoped I wouldn't have to.

"What's going on?" Gail said as Tommy was getting out from his chair. He grabbed my arm and led me away to an empty table.

"Don't be long, baby, Mom and Dad are expecting us at seven," Gail said, making sure I heard.

"What the hell, Justine?"

"I should ask you the same thing. It hasn't even been two months and you're already meeting her parents. You two are—" I stopped talking. I didn't want to think about him with someone else. Even at this moment, I loved him completely. I wanted him back and I knew that he would want me once he knew my news.

"Justine, it's over. I thought you'd get it. Damn, do I have to spell it out for you? O-V-E-R." He glanced at Gail, who was watching us.

"Tommy, I have something important to tell you."

"I don't love you anymore."

The words hurt. For the first time since the night we had made love, I let those words in. I had been feeling the meaning of those words for months, but now, the truth was here, cold and bitter tasting. It *was* over.

"I've got to go. I'm not going to be late." He slid the chair back from the table and as he pulled away from me, I knew I could love enough for the both of us and our baby.

"Wait!" I grabbed his shirt. "I'm pregnant. I'm going to have your child," I said. He sat back down and I knew that he was going to be mine again.

"You're lying. Trying to trap me."

"Trap you? This is your baby! We can be a family. Tommy, you're going to be a father."

"Look, it's over and you can play all the games you want."

Tommy walked away and I stood up from the table, rage bubbling inside me. I yelled Tommy's name and everyone in the place listened as I called him every terrible name I could think of. I made my way out of the grill without breaking down, but by the time I reached the sidewalk, I was shaking and crying.

For many years after that night, I wished love was something you could turn off. I don't know why, but I still loved Tommy. I even made up excuses for the way he treated me that night. But that was the dream.

The reality was that my aunt and uncle were tired of me living with them, and I wasn't going to be able to hide the pregnancy for much longer. I thought about Samuel. I wondered what kind of father he would be and whether I could love him and build a life like the one I had dreamed about with Tommy. All that didn't matter, what mattered was giving you a home and a family.

At the end of January, Samuel came back into town for another job, and he called me the night he got in. The next morning, we met at the doughnut shop for coffee.

Samuel in his tattered jeans, navy flannel shirt, and dirty tool bag looked awkward on top of the red cushion-topped stool with its shiny chrome pedestal.

"Hi," I said. His eyes seemed sad and he turned his body back to face the counter.

"Want some coffee? Doughnut?" he said not looking at me.

"Yeah, I'll have both. What kind do you have?"

"Raspberry filled."

"That'll be great. Samuel, we need to talk." I guided his face with my hand to look at me. I wanted to see his face when I told him. The way things went with Tommy, I decided to do something different. Be quick. If Samuel didn't want you or me, I wanted to know right off.

"Samuel, I'm pregnant," I said and braced myself for the ugliness.

He smiled. For the first time since I had known him, he smiled. "A baby?"

"Yes."

"Really?" Samuel stood up, and I nodded and he hugged me close to him. He kissed me lightly. I didn't kiss back. I was shocked by his reaction. He said, "Are you okay? I didn't squeeze too hard?"

"I'm fine. Samuel, are you happy about this?"

"Yes! I thought ... I thought you were breaking it off with me. I've loved you from the moment I saw you. I tried to tell you. Remember, that first night while we were dancing." He pulled me into him again and kissed my neck and whispered, "Forever."

I couldn't speak. He was not turning away from me—he wanted me, baby and all.

"A baby." He sat down on the stool and sipped his coffee. "God, I hope if it's a girl she looks like you." He brushed his hair away from his eye and turned to the counter again. He was a man on the outside, but at that moment I saw a boy. I kissed his hand and held it.

He reached down the counter, past two napkin holders and grabbed the cashier's pen. He wrote on his napkin and pushed it in front of me. I looked down at the napkin and it read, Marry me?

"Can I see the pen?" I wrote my answer on the napkin and placed in on top of his doughnut. The letters Y-E-S made him smile again.

. . .

SAMUEL and I got married on Valentine's Day 1965, less than a month after I told him about you. There weren't many people at the wedding. My aunt and uncle came, my uncle celebrated the fact I'd be moving out more than my marriage. I didn't have anyone walk me down the aisle.

Samuel's father showed up for the reception we had at the Ruritan Club. He was drunk. At the entry way of the hall, Samuel pushed his father in the chest a couple of times and then led him to the door. From the window, I could see his father yelling and stumbling his way to his car.

Samuel told me little about his family. I told him all about my parents, but never mentioned anyone else. It was kind of this unspoken thing between Samuel and me—we didn't want to know much about each other's past.

Oh, Lacy, Samuel and I were happy. In the beginning, he had enough love for both of us. Samuel said it would be best for you if I quit work. So by April, I was at home waiting for him each night.

After you came, I grew to love him. I bet you don't remember our Sunday afternoons during the summers. You were two and three. Those were good times. We'd go to the park and take turns pushing you in the swing. And after, we'd go get ice cream.

Then everything changed.

Tommy came to the house a couple of weeks before Christmas of '68. You were about three and a half years old. When I opened the door, it took me a minute to realize it was him. His hair was longer, so it was wavy instead of tightly curled, and he looked like one of those men in the business suit catalogs. The smile, the Tommy Franco weapon, exposed who he was. I was so in shock, he had to ask if he could come in.

He slid his coat off, and I noticed the chest and back of a man. The black turtleneck sweater pulled tightly against his body. He looked good. I got ahold of myself and pointed to the couch and asked how he was doing. We discussed his parents and other friends back in Reidsville. He said he had graduated from Duke and mentioned a couple of promising job interviews he had coming up.

At first, our conversation was just about small things like that. All the feelings I had for him came flooding back to me. It was strange, I felt like no time had passed since the last time I had seen him. Although I hadn't forgotten how he'd treated me, I had forgiven him long ago.

Tommy kept looking at you. He even played with you on the floor a bit. When I watched the two of you together, I was overwhelmed. For many nights after I'd told him about you, I cried and wished he would have married me. That moment, as you two played together, had been something I had only seen in my dreams. Tommy was sitting alone on the couch when Samuel came home and you were playing on the floor with your blocks. Samuel and the other guys on his team were laid off from the welding company and they had stopped off to drink to their lost jobs. That's why he was home early. Unfortunately, I didn't know this until much later.

Samuel slipped off his work boots at the door and yelled my name. I came from the kitchen with a plate full of cheese and crackers. He looked tired and his work clothes smelled like beer. His eyes asked, Who is this *man* in *my* living room?

"Samuel, this is Tommy Franco," I said, nearly dropping the plate on the coffee table. Samuel gave a nod and walked to the refrigerator.

"How do you two know each other?" Samuel asked coming back from the kitchen with two opened beers. He offered one to Tommy.

"No, thanks. We're friends from high school," Tommy said and smiled. He could sell anything with that smile, I thought.

"Friends." Samuel tipped the first beer up and didn't stop

until it was gone.

"Tommy knew my parents," I said, wondering what that had to do with anything—it was something to fill the painful silence that had taken over.

Tommy looked at me and I smiled and got on the floor with you. I needed something to keep my hands busy. There had been little glimpses of the way Samuel loved me before this day. If a bag boy at the grocery store stared too long at me, Samuel got upset. I learned quickly not to smile back at anyone who looked too long my way.

Once, the neighbor one street over brought me some apples from his grandfather's farm and Samuel came home from work just in time to see the neighbor touching my shoulder. He was just one of those touchy people, you know the ones who can't help but put their hands on you when they talk. I tried to assure Samuel of the innocence of what happened. After we got inside, he pinned me against the front door. His grip was so tight it left imprints of his fingers on my upper arms. He kept yelling over and over that I would leave him for someone else and why did I do this to him. Deep down, I knew something was wrong, but I also knew there was nothing I could do. That night after dinner, he apologized. Days later, when the bruises on my arms turned colors, he kissed them and said he was sorry again. He loved me so much.

"Tommy, it was great of you to stop by. Good luck with those job interviews," I said trying to get Tommy to leave. It was time for him to leave, way past time.

You stood beside the coffee table and played with your blocks. You put some blocks into a plastic pot and called it soup. With a block in each hand, you hit the wooden coffee table with a rhythm that only a three-year-old would make, loud and constant.

"Yeah, good luck with your *job* interviews," Samuel said and started on the other beer.

"Lacy, stir your soup," I said.

"No, I cutting potatoes now," you said and hit the table harder and faster.

"Dammit, girl, stop it!" Samuel said and grabbed the blocks from your hands. His beer spilled all over your blocks, you, and the table. You cried and Samuel said, "Now look what you made me do!"

"It's not her fault, she's just a little girl," Tommy said. It was one of those things that should be thought and not said out loud. By Tommy's face, I could tell he was surprised that the words had slipped out.

"Who the hell do you think you are?" Samuel said.

"No one." Tommy stood up from the couch and stared at Samuel. He turned my way. "Justine, I need to know one thing before I leave," Tommy said as he put his arms into his coat.

I wanted him to leave before things got worse. *Just leave, Tommy, leave.*

"When you saw me four years ago at the grill, is what you told me true? Because if it is, I damn well have a say here." Tommy buttoned up his coat and stood by the door and he wasn't budging until I answered him.

"Tommy, I ..." My eyes filled with tears and I know it was the way I said Tommy's name that set Samuel off. I never knew you could show love without even meaning to.

"You don't have any fucking say here. This is my house. I want you out. Now!" Samuel said pushing Tommy's shoulder.

"I've got a say in how my daughter's raised, asshole. Don't ever touch me again!" Tommy said and pushed Samuel back.

"Just go, Tommy, go!" I yelled and picked you up and held you close.

"What the fuck are you talking about?" Samuel said to Tommy, but he looked at me.

"Samuel, he's wrong. Lacy is yours. Yours."

"Justine, that's not what you told me when you found out you were pregnant. Just look at her. Goddammit, you can tell she's mine. I have rights as her father."

Samuel flew into a rage. Everything that happened next is a blur. Samuel and Tommy fell onto the coffee table and flattened it. I remember trying to pull them away from each other, and the next thing I remember, you were crawling over to me on the floor and Samuel and Tommy were gone.

Late that night, Samuel came back home. In the morning, I made breakfast and tried to be as normal as possible. We never did talk about that night. I thought at the time that not talking about it, hiding from what had happened was the best thing. But what I didn't realize was, when you let your mind go unanswered, it eats away at your life. And Samuel was never the same after that night. There were very few times I would see glimpses of the Samuel I married. But as quick as those glimpses came, they were gone again. Like an animal afraid to come out of his cave.

Tommy wrote me after he left that day. You have that letter, I think. Samuel loved me and had been a good husband and father before Tommy had come. So, I wrote a letter to Tommy telling him that he was not the father and to not come around again. But the damage was done. Samuel could tell how much I had cared for Tommy, and still did. The seed of doubt about you had been planted. He drank more and the hitting began. It happened only two or three times the year after, but then, it got worse.

I tried to leave him. Two years after Tommy's visit, you and I left Samuel. It was only for a weekend. I went to Reidsville to see Tommy. His folks said he had gotten married and moved away. They didn't shut the door in my face, but I could tell they didn't want me around.

I knew I wasn't strong enough to be on my own and be a mother to you. So, I went back, and Samuel made me regret leaving.

I'm not as strong as you, Lacy. The night you left, I went into your room because I was afraid. And it wasn't of Samuel. What he did to me became part of life for me. I was afraid that I would lose you. I had a nightmare. You were trapped in a burning building and I couldn't get to you. The flames leapt out at me every time I tried to run to the building to rescue you. It's probably every mother's nightmare, but for me it was real. I knew I was sick, and I guess the weight of what your life was going to be without me carried over into my dreams.

I went up to your room to watch you sleep. When you were a baby, I watched your face as you slept. Peaceful, about the most peaceful thing I knew. That night, although you were thirteen, you were a baby all over again. I watched your face and felt so calm, I fell asleep beside you.

I HOPE what I have written helps you understand your life better. My dream was to tell you these things over coffee, two women talking about life. But, honey, our dreams don't always come true. Life changes.

One thing I have learned, it's better to live in life than to live in your dreams. I hope you understand what that means. It took me a long time to figure it out.

I wish I could tell you the truth about your father, but I don't know myself. I was careless to do what I did with Tommy and Samuel. But when I think of you, I know that something beautiful came out of what I did.

I love you with all my heart, and please forgive me for everything I failed you in.

14

The windshield wipers flapped back and forth, attempting to clear the rain so Annie could see. The wiper on Annie's side was falling apart; it reminded me of those blue-tailed lizards at Butch's house—with each swipe of the blade, its black rubber tail wiggled.

When Annie pulled into the hospital parking lot, it seemed that we had been in the car for just a second. I stepped out of the van into a puddle and the water went over my ankle, soaking the bottom of my jeans. Through the hospital hallways, my tennis shoe squeaked and sloshed.

Last night, Annie hadn't asked me about what was in the envelope. When I'd finished reading the letter, I covered myself up with the blanket and was more confused than the day I'd left home. I thought my mother would have the answers, but she didn't. She was someone to be angry at when I ran away—after reading her letter—she was someone else. My head hurt. I wished I had known she was sick, maybe I wouldn't have left her alone, maybe I would have made her run away with me. And I wished she had told me about Tommy; he wasn't perfect, but I knew he had to be my father. Why had my mother stayed with Samuel? Why?

Before I went to sleep, I told Annie through the covers that she could read the letter. I wanted her to read it. Someone needed to give me answers, tell me the truth. Maybe Annie would read something I missed.

When we reached my mother's hospital room, my shoe stopped squeaking, but the bottom of my jeans was cold and clung to my leg. The first bed where the raven-haired lady had been was empty. With the curtain pulled back and my mother's bed in sight, Annie and I stood just inside the room and looked at my sleeping mother.

"I'm going to go call Roger and see how things are at the farm. You need this time with your mother. Don't forget, say what's in your heart." Annie gave me a hug and headed down the hall.

I'd made it to the middle of the room when a nurse came in.

"Hi, just going to check her drip, and then I'll be out of the way for your visit," she said. The nurse hovered over my mother. She checked the bottle connected to the tube that ran to her arm, pulled the blankets up around her shoulders and leaned in and listened to my mother.

"She's cold. I'm going to get a couple of warm blankets. I'll be right back," the nurse said. Her pantyhose swished as she walked by me.

"Mom." I walked toward her. When I reached the bed, I called her again. Her pink eyelids opened and she smiled.

"Lacy, did you get ... my letter ... from Liz?"

"Yeah, I read it."

"I'm sorry ... I wasn't—"

"I'm sorry for leaving you." I leaned over the bed and tried to hug her. Her hands pressed on my sides, she was trying to hug me back. I pulled back and wiped my eyes.

"I'm so tired Lacy," she said and closed her eyes.

I stepped away to the window to give her a rest. There were so many questions I wanted to ask her. With so little strength, it would take all day for just one of my questions to be answered. I watched the rain bounce off the roof. Little puddles collected between the tan, beige, and rose pebbles, making one large watery sheet across the roof. The nurse came back with the extra blanket and slowly placed it on my mother.

"Honey," the nurse said and looked at me. "She's gone."

"Gone? What do you mean by gone?"

I shouted her name. Her eyes didn't open.

"I'm sorry," the nurse said and moved toward me.

I shouted again, turned back to the window and slapped my hands and arms against the glass. I think I cried, but I just remember yelling the word *no*. The nurse said something to me, but I couldn't understand.

Annie ran into the room, grabbed me, and held me tight. I couldn't stop shouting. I pushed Annie away and knelt beside the bed at my mother's feet. The nurse came over. I thought she was going to move me, so I buried my face in the blankets and clutched my mother's legs.

"It's okay, honey, you stay there. I'm going to put this rail down so you can say goodbye." In one motion, the nurse put the metal rail down alongside the bed. Before she left the room, she touched Annie's arm and said she'd be right out in the hall.

I remembered covering my mother's legs at home on the couch. She would fall asleep and pull the blanket around her chin leaving her feet and legs uncovered. I'd take the red-and-black checkered blanket off the back of the couch and cover the rest of her. When the tassels of blanket fell to the carpet, she'd say, "You're a good girl, Lacy." I looked at my mother's pale face and waited for her to thank me.

The smell of alcohol—fresh, like a bottle had just been

opened and stale, like when it oozes out someone's pores—filled the air. He stood there. I turned around to find Annie; she was waiting for me in the chair. Slowly, I turned back toward him and lifted my gaze across the bed and stared at his hands. I didn't want to see him. His fingers were laced together and rested near his belt buckle.

With heavy steps, he walked to the top of the bed, to my mother's face. His fingers cupped the back of her head, and he kissed her forehead. He whispered something in my mother's ear and then I heard something I had never heard before.

Samuel Mitchell cried. It wasn't a loud cry; it was muffled, like crying into a pillow. His back and shoulders moved in little pulses as he held my mother's head next to his.

"Get out," he said. I didn't move. "You caused this. You made her sick." Samuel released my mother's head and stood. "Get out!" He grabbed the metal rail on the other side of the bed.

"Lacy, let's go," Annie said and tugged at my arm, trying to lead me to the door.

"I didn't get to say goodbye," I said, not directly looking at him. Annie pulled me to the end of the bed and then switched to pulling my arm closest to the door. Samuel Mitchell and I were face-to-face.

"You don't deserve to do anything," he said and looked at my mother's body.

"I deserve it more than you do!"

His open hand came across my face, and I fell back against the wall. Annie tried to stop him from hitting me again, but he pushed her shoulders, and she fell down right beside me.

"This shit ate her up 'cause you left. I hope you're happy. You killed her!" His kick didn't hurt as much as his words. I rolled my body into a ball.

The kicks stopped and I shot up onto my feet. "I hate you! I hate you!" I pushed him in the chest. He went still as my push registered, and then his hands were around my neck and my feet were off the floor.

"I ... hate—" I tried to say the words again, but there wasn't enough air to finish. The room was silent, everything was the same, but I heard nothing, it was like I was watching a silent movie. His hands didn't hurt my neck anymore and warmth tickled over my body. I blinked and a herd of people in green and white surrounded me. They pulled Samuel away from me; he let go, and I slid down the wall. Two nurses shepherded Annie and I out of the room and into the elevator.

NEITHER ONE OF us spoke on the ride back to the hotel. My back stiffened before we reached the room. I had felt this kind of tightness many times before, and I knew what would be on my back in a few days. The marks would fade, but I kept thinking about his words. If they were true, then I had hurt my mother more than Samuel Mitchell ever had.

"Let me see your back," Annie said. I put my hand on the spot that hurt the most. She lifted up my shirt and ran her fingers over the place where he'd kicked me. My body shivered and pulled away from her touch.

"Are you hungry?" Annie asked and released my shirt.

"No."

"I'm so sorry, Lacy. For everything. Dammit, you shouldn't have to go through this," Annie said, quickly making up my bed. She patted her hand against the floral bedspread. I sat down, and she hugged me tight. I closed my eyes and sank into her.

When I opened my eyes, it was late afternoon. Annie had tucked a blanket over me and the water from the shower was running. A thought came to me: I would never see my mother again. Never talk to her and never be able to say I was sorry for hurting her. I pulled the blanket over my head and wrapped it tight around myself. I wanted to stay in the darkness. I wished for something to happen to me like a lightning strike, heart attack, or an attack by a giant spider, something that would stop the pain. Wrapped in my blanket cocoon, I cried.

"It's not your fault, Lacy. God, it's not your fault," Annie said and sat on the bed. "Your mother died of ovarian cancer. You did not cause that. Don't you listen to a word he said." Annie stood. I heard her suitcase zipper. After she got dressed, she sat again on the bed and explained how my mother hadn't gone to the doctor in time to get treatment and how ovarian cancer didn't hurt until it had really spread. Even though Annie tried her best to make me feel better, I knew that I had caused my mother great pain in leaving her, and I couldn't help but think that her worry made her die faster.

"Lacy, I need you to listen. I talked to Mr. Williamson this morning. You received a letter from Tommy Franco at the farm."

She pulled the blanket out from around my head. My eyes were heavy and wanted to shut again. Annie looked at my face and went to the bathroom for toilet paper.

"The letter sounds like it's him." She handed me the toilet paper. I wiped my nose. "I hope you don't mind, I had Roger read it to me over the phone. Tommy gave a phone number and suggested you call him. I know this is a lot to take in at one time. But I think you need to call him as soon as you can."

I put my head under the blanket again.

WHEN I WOKE AGAIN, the room was dark. I thought my head was still under the blanket. I unraveled myself and went to the bathroom. Annie had put a note in the sink that she had gone out to get food for us and she would be back in fifteen minutes. I pulled all the things I had found in my mother's closet from my duffel bag. I laid everything out in front of me. The clipping had ripped in two, so I placed the halves together. I reread his letter and placed the black-and-white photo of him and my mother on top of the letter. She looked so happy. I unfolded the small bit of square paper and stared at the overlapping lines of color that weaved through the center of the paper. He had used blue, green, and red ink, and by going over the circle, changing his direction slightly with each time around, he had made a beautiful design. I touched the cursive *T* he had written. I had found Tommy Franco, found him on the same day I'd lost my mother.

I GAVE the operator my first name. The longer the phone rang, the more I wanted to hang up. And a then a deep, scratchy voice said hello. The voice didn't match the pictures I had. When you dream about someone for so long, to actually hear them, well, they sound fake.

"Collect call from Lacy, will you accept the charges?"

I waited. Would he accept the charges? At that moment, that question seemed bigger than the phone call. Would he accept my whole life? Me? The truth?

"Yes, I will."

I held onto the phone—not speaking, just listening.

"Hello?" he said.

"Hi." All this time spent thinking about him, and I didn't even know what to say. What to talk about?

"I got your letter. Well, my parents got it and then forwarded it on to me. That's why it took so long to answer you."

"Oh." I couldn't form a thought.

"I met you once. I don't know if you remember or not. God, you must have been three or four years old."

"Yeah, I remember." I remembered a lot about that day. Though, now it was hard to figure out what was my memory and what I'd read from my mother's letter. It didn't matter what was what, really. I knew what had happened that day.

"How's your mother?"

I felt my mouth open, but nothing came out. I saw my mother lying in the hospital bed with her pink eyelids and milky skin and tears came again.

"Are you okay? Lacy, are you there?"

"My mother's gone."

"Gone? Where?"

"She died today. Cancer."

"I'm so sorry."

"I ran away looking for you. I didn't even know she was sick." The hotel door came open and Annie stepped inside with McDonald's. She mouthed the word *who* and pointed to the phone. I picked up the paper that Annie had written Tommy Franco's phone number on. She nodded.

"You ran away? Are you safe now?"

"Yes, my friend Annie is helping me."

"I'm sorry about your mother. She was a good woman. Someday soon, I would like to meet you."

"I'd like to meet you too." I heard a little boy's voice in the background. *Daddy, Daddy.* His voice made me angry, and I didn't know why. I had thought about Tommy having children, but never wanted that fact to be true—or I guess I had only dreamed about me being that child.

"Well then, that's decided. You should go and rest and I have to see what this little guy wants. Lacy, I'm so glad you found me. I want to get to know you, and I know we have a lot to talk about."

"Yeah."

15

They put my mother in the ground the day before my fourteenth birthday. It didn't look natural to have the coffin hovering above the ground and the fake green grass on top of the dirt around the hole. The sun in the middle of the sky beat down on us, and everyone wiped their faces, whether it was tears or sweat. When I looked at the box that held my mother, the gold handles along the side of the coffin blinded me.

My mind went to the burying beetle. They come at night because of the smell of death and lay their eggs near the corpse. At first, their young feed on the parents' vomit left in a hole in the dead body. When the young grow, they feed on the corpse. The behavior of the beetles was natural, but it made me feel sick. I wanted someone to do something to protect her from them. I looked again at the shiny gold handles of the hard case that held her and hoped that the beetles couldn't get into that man-made metal shell.

Samuel Mitchell sat in a chair across from me. He looked like a marionette without the strings. His back curved, his head, slumped and his hands, rested on his knees, lifelessly. Each time he shifted the metal folding chair creaked. I had never seen him dressed in a suit before with his hair slicked back. Once, when the pastor spoke, Samuel looked at the coffin at the same time I did. Our eyes locked. His face seemed old, dark rings were under his eyes and his cheeks were sunken in. I wasn't afraid of him at that moment, I felt sorry for him. His chin dropped toward his chest, and I was mad at myself for feeling any pity for him.

Annie grabbed my hand and squeezed it, letting me know she was there. The pastor said some words and everyone joined in. I had heard the beginning before, *The Lord is my shepherd.* I lifted my head and looked around at the people saying the words. Some had their eyes closed, some people were crying, and some just looked like zombies. I wondered who these people were. I recognized a few neighbors. One tall man with dark sunglasses smiled at me. It wasn't a this-is-fun kind of smile. It was gentler, like an it's-gonna-be-okay smile. He was about three people behind Samuel, so I could only see his head and shoulders.

When the service was over, Samuel sat hunched over in the chair. All the other people made their way up the hill to the gravel road where the cars were parked. Everyone kept hugging me and telling me what a good woman my mother was or that they would miss her. Liz, the neighbor— the only person I truly knew— cried when she hugged me. When she said she would miss my mother, I believed her.

I looked down the hill and two guys in jeans and T-shirts rode up on a golf cart. I saw handles of tools sticking out of the back of the cart. They stood at a distance talking to each other and glancing up at Samuel Mitchell. I guessed they were the closers, and they were waiting for Samuel to leave, so they could put the dirt on top of my mother. The flash of the orange-and-black beetle popped into my head again. I shook it off and thought about the gold handles again and how strong the metal would be for my mother.

"Lacy," the man with the sunglasses said as he held his hand out for me to shake. I watched him slip off his sunglasses, fold them up and put them into his pocket. I placed my hand into his. He continued, "Tommy Franco. I'm sorry about your mother. After you called a few days ago—I knew I wanted to come."

"It's really nice to meet you," I said and looked for Annie so she could see that he was real. She and Liz were talking beside Liz's car. Annie gave me a nod when I looked her way, the nod meant *I'll be there in just a minute*. Didn't she know that this was him?

I turned back to this man I had searched for and studied him. All my dreams were real, he *was* real. He was not as tall as Samuel Mitchell, but he was sturdier. His hair was cut close to his head and strips of gray rode over his ears. I tried to think of something else to say. But nothing came to my mind; I just wanted to look at him.

"I'm going to be in town for a few days. I wanted to know if you would like to get together and talk?"

"Yeah, I'd like that. Come here, I want you to meet my friend." I walked toward Annie and Liz. I glanced back to make sure he hadn't disappeared. He smiled.

Liz leaned on her car while Annie talked and when we came up, Annie didn't stop the conversation. So, I interrupted.

"Annie, this is Tommy Franco," I said, which stopped her talking. I watched Annie's shocked face as she stared at my father. While they talked, I noticed Tommy's feet, black fancy shoes with tassels; his hands, long fingers, just like me, and on his left hand there was a plain gold band; his eyes, not chocolate brown like mine, they were milky brown with yellow spokes that came out from his pupil. I must have been staring too hard because he glanced over at me and grinned while he continued talking to Annie.

Ashamed for looking too long, I turned my head. Samuel Mitchell was still in the chair. The workers had moved closer to the graveside, and their shovels were in their hands. The pastor stood at the end of the hole. Samuel stood quickly and the metal chair collapsed. The pastor touched his arm, trying to make him feel better, I think. Samuel jerked his arm away, yelled something, and started up the grassy hill.

"Lacy, are you listening?" Annie tapped my shoulder.

"What?"

"Well, that answers that question. Tommy wants to know if we would like to meet him for dinner."

"You'll have to pick where. I just drove straight to the cemetery," Tommy said.

Liz spoke. "There's a diner in town, One for the Road. It's greasy grill food, but they won't kick you out for taking up table space. And their mushroom Swiss burgers are great."

"Okay, then. One for the Road, it is. Let's say around six," Annie said.

"Son of a bitch! What the fuck are you doing here?" Samuel Mitchell said. He had appeared right behind Tommy.

Tommy turned and faced Samuel. I was right—Samuel stood a whole head taller than Tommy. Annie led me to the van and whispered, "Get in."

"I was saying goodbye," Tommy said before he put his sunglasses on and walked toward his car.

"Goddamn you, stay away from her. Stay the fuck away from her!" Samuel yelled at Tommy's back.

As if he didn't even hear the words, Tommy looked at Annie and said, "See you at six."

Tommy slammed his Jeep door. Annie locked her door and

told me to do the same. I watched Samuel. He kicked the gravel and walked to his car. As we drove the van out, we passed him, on my side. His forehead wrinkled and his eyes were empty. I knew that face, and I knew what was inside him would come out.

∾

Summers are hard for me, lots of memories. Thoughts of blackberries with milk and sugar and blueberry muffins take away some bitterness.

We didn't plant the blackberries; they just grow wild along the fence on one side of Annie's property. Last summer, we had berries as big around as my thumb.

We haven't had a real rain in weeks. The last rain that did any good was the middle of April right round the time I got your first letter. Annie says if we don't get rain soon, this year's crop will be in trouble. She's thinking about putting in an irrigation system for next year.

I got your postcard last week. Annie pointed out to me that the Kewpie doll on the card was a scientist. Very cute, thanks. I really do want to meet you too. How about the middle of July? I'll mail the rest of this to you no later than the end of June. And after you finish, I'll understand if you don't want to meet.

Lacy

16

One For The Road smelled like burnt burgers mixed with onions. Road signs were nailed to the walls and miniature black roads that led nowhere were painted on the floor. All the booths were up against the glass windows. Annie always liked sitting in booths, never tables, so I slid into a booth near the door. The back of my legs clung to the orange vinyl as I scooted in to make room for Annie.

"What time is it?"

"Five minutes past the last time you asked." Annie scanned her menu.

"Annie, please."

"Five to six."

"What if he doesn't come?"

"He'll be here, Lacy."

I leaned into the window and looked for Tommy's Jeep down the street. Through the glass, the sun warmed my shoulder almost to a burning. I looked behind me and then back down the way I had looked before, and there he was. He seemed younger without his suit. The fringe on his cutoffs hung unevenly around his legs and his T-shirt was wet with sweat. His sunglasses reflected the sun and he smiled at me and I waved. A string of cowbells rang as a gush of hot air came in with Tommy.

He sat down across from Annie and me and wiped his forehead with a napkin.

"God, it's hot here."

"It's not this hot in Ohio, is it?" Annie asked.

"No, I'd melt here. I think I've lost five pounds today." Tommy smiled and I realized the truth of what my mother had written. Tommy's face lit up when he smiled, and it made everything seem like it would be okay.

"Where in Ohio?" I asked.

"Columbus," Annie and Tommy answered together. Tommy looked at Annie.

"How did you know where he lived?" I asked Annie.

Annie glanced at the menu and said, "Mr. Williamson read me the return address from his letter."

"Are you hungry?" Tommy asked me.

"Not really."

An old woman with a long gray braid and a name tag that read Nettie came to take our order. She asked what we wanted and then took the orders of two tables in the center of the diner and rushed back to the kitchen. I watched Nettie work for a while because I knew what I wanted to say, but I was afraid of the answer. I decided to push the words out, and then I figured, everything would be over.

"Why did you leave me?" I asked Tommy, but kept my eyes on Nettie.

"I didn't leave you, Lacy. I came back, but—" Nettie brought our drinks and stood for a moment like she was waiting for Tommy to finish what he was saying. He said nothing.

"Your food will be up in a few," she said and walked away.

"Lacy, God, I don't know where to begin." He raked his fingers through his hair. "What did your mother tell you?" He spoke again before I could answer. "No, wait, I'll tell you what happened. I was such a jerk." He put sugar in his coffee. "Young and stupid ... and just a jerk." Tommy shook his head. "I was finishing my first year of college. I thought I had the world, by the—" He stopped himself and stirred his coffee.

"When your mother told me she was pregnant, I didn't believe her." He brought his lips to the cup and pulled away quickly. "Too hot. Right after I graduated, I went to visit Justine and you. On the phone you said you remembered that visit."

Annie wiped the condensation off her glass with her napkin and said, "What made you go back to see Justine after college?"

"I don't know exactly. Maybe I realized what a great thing I had blown with her. And, I ... I also wanted to see if there really was a baby, a child that I had created. That day was a disaster. It went nothing like I thought it would."

"Do you remember you played with me?" I asked.

"Yes, we built towers out of your wooden blocks. When I saw you, my gut told me that you were my daughter. But things went downhill after Samuel came home."

"Why didn't you go back or pursue it legally?" Annie said.

"Justine wrote a letter shortly after that visit stating that there was no way Lacy was my daughter. So, I dropped it. Now, I see what a mistake that was." Tommy looked at me and I felt like crying. He continued, "I didn't want to cause any more trouble. I moved on because Justine was happy. And she deserved to be treated right."

"Treated right? Do you know that Samuel Mitchell was abusive?" Annie said, and I could feel the tension in her voice. I thought about the word *abusive*, it was too small of word to describe what it meant.

"Did he hurt you, Lacy?" Tommy said and stared at me.

"Did he hurt me?" I repeated his question. How could I answer that? He hurt me, I wanted shout. Why hadn't Tommy ever thought of that before? When Samuel threw him on the table, wasn't that proof of the person Samuel was?

Nettie placed our burgers and fries in front of us and scurried away with two plates of food still balanced on her arm. I stared at the oval plate with maroon trim and tried to keep the anger from spilling out of me.

"Yeah, he hurt me." I looked Tommy right in the eyes and said, "But he hurt my mom even more." I watched and waited. His face changed, and he didn't look at me anymore. Annie rubbed my back as I kept my gaze on Tommy, waiting for an answer— waiting for his reason for why he didn't save me.

The cowbells clattered against the door, and Samuel Mitchell stumbled in. He fell into a table, scattering plates, glasses, and bits of uneaten hamburger to the floor. He straightened himself and stood in front of our booth. His T-shirt was stained with hamburger grease and his jeans hung on him like he was a clothes hanger.

"So, what's goin' on here?" Samuel slammed his hands against the table and leaned in toward me. The blood vessels in his hands looked like crawling caterpillars.

"Nothing that's any of your business." Tommy stood, his knees hit the table and the plates rattled.

"Fuck you," Samuel said and pushed Tommy back into the booth.

Tommy rose again. Samuel's hands went behind his back. Nettie raised her head and stopped picking up pieces of glass from the floor.

A loud thundering sound came from Samuel's hand, which he held high toward the ceiling. Everyone screamed, and my eyes traced his arm to his hand, and then I saw the gun.

"Shut up, everybody. Shut the fuck up." Samuel spun around, talking to no one but talking to everyone. "Get out of here." He pointed the gun in Nettie's face. "And take 'em all with you."

She stood with shattered glass around her feet and looked dazed.

"Goddamn it, now!" Samuel yelled.

Nettie startled and moved quickly, herding the customers, the cook, and herself out the front door.

Samuel pulled an overturned chair next to the booth and sat down. The stench of alcohol settled on our table. "So, I see you've met your reeeeal daddy." Samuel opened the chamber of the gun. Tommy moved in his seat, and Samuel flipped the chamber closed and placed the tip of the gun on Tommy's temple.

"For God's sake," Annie said.

Samuel removed the gun and turned toward Annie.

"Get out. This isn't your business."

"I'm not leaving Lacy."

"You wanna make a goddamn bet?" Samuel pointed the gun at Annie's chest.

"Go, Annie, please. Just go," I said and pushed her out of the booth.

The cowbells hit against the glass and the sound seemed louder than all the other times. It was just me and my fathers. I looked at their faces. They did look similar; I could see why my mother went to Samuel so soon after Tommy. Samuel was thinner than I'd ever seen him, so his face was very sharp. Tommy's face was rounder and he looked softer because of that. I thought about my mother and wondered if she was watching.

I glanced out the window and saw Annie's worried face. A crowd had formed and sirens screamed in the distance. Samuel didn't have long before the police would be here. I didn't know what Samuel wanted; I wondered if he even knew what he wanted.

"She was a good woman," Samuel said, breaking the silence.

Tommy and I looked at each other.

"I loved her. I loved her like nothing else in my life. But she didn't love me"—he paused and rubbed his fingers across the edge of the table—"like she loved you." Samuel waved the gun at Tommy not stopping on any part of him.

"Why don't you put the gun down, and we could talk—"

"I don't want to fucking talk." Samuel pulled the hammer back.

Tommy pushed the gun away. Another thunder.

I closed my eyes and my ears rang. When I opened my eyes, Tommy was hunched over the table. I was next. I looked for Annie in the crowd. She was gone. Red and blue lights swirled.

I turned back to face Samuel. This was it. I'd run away from this man only to have him kill me like I'd always known he would.

"Get over here," Samuel said, grabbed my arm and jerked me out of the booth. When he released his grip, I fell into the glass that Nettie hadn't finished cleaning. I felt a ripping and burning on my palm. I looked down at a jagged piece of glass that stuck out of my flesh. I pulled it out and pressed the bottom of my T-shirt against the cut.

Samuel tucked the gun in his pants and put both hands on his hips.

"Stand up," he yelled. I stood up. Samuel Mitchell didn't need a gun to make me do want he wanted. I guessed he was going to beat me to death.

"It wasn't supposed to be like this," he said, glancing around the diner and staring at Tommy's hunched-over body.

"Why did she die? Why?" Samuel yelled.

I didn't know why it happened. Cancer killed her, I killed her, he killed her. It didn't matter—she was gone, and I knew better than to answer him.

His body swayed and he put his hand down on a table to steady himself. He stared at me, like he was looking for something he had lost. "You don't look like your momma." He closed his eyes. "Why?" he said again, this time almost crying.

There was something in his voice I'd never noticed before: love. Even with all the pain he'd caused my mother, he still loved her. We looked at each other for what seemed to be a lifetime.

A crash came from the kitchen. Annie stepped out from the kitchen and said, "Please don't hurt her, please don't hurt her." She walked slowly in Samuel's direction and repeated the words again. He grabbed the gun, pulled the hammer back, and aimed for Annie. I ran and jumped on Samuel.

Thunder.

I lay on top of Samuel Mitchell and warm liquid spread across my belly. I looked at his face and he looked into my eyes, a tear rolled down his cheek.

Everything went dark.

17

A black thread peeked out from the bandage on my hand, it reminded me of a carpenter ant's leg. I peeled back the white tape and stared at the row of dots with two legs. Fifteen stitches on the outside and six on the inside. I sat back on the hard couch cushions lined with gray ridges and dotted with blue flecks. In the vending machine, a bag of chips hung by one corner; a little shake and the chips would be free from the metal corkscrew. But I wasn't hungry. Annie had left me a Coke on the table. I didn't drink it. I ran my finger over the tops of the stitches. It tickled my skin and made me feel sick at the same time.

"You'd better cover that back up, you don't want it to get infected." A man in a dark-blue police uniform slid my Coke over and sat on the table in front of me. I placed the bandage back over the black thread and pressed the tape against my skin.

"I need to talk with you. Where's the lady that was with you earlier?

"She'll be right back." The man's face seemed too young for his body, I would have guessed he was sixteen, but with the police uniform and his height, I added another four or five years onto his age. There was a long pause before he spoke again.

"I'll wait until she gets back before we talk." He stood up from the table and put some change into the vending machine.

I knew what he wanted. He wanted me to tell him about what happened at One for the Road. It had only been a few hours ago, but when I tried to remember, it seemed like a fuzzy dream. Some parts I didn't remember at all, like the man's button-down shirt I now wore or how I got to the hospital. I did remember the doctor numbing my hand and his needle threading through my skin, sewing the gash closed.

"You want some chips? I got an extra bag."

"No," I said.

A heavy woman in a khaki skirt and tennis shoes came down the hallway.

"Officer Jefferson," she called, and the uniformed man walked to meet her. They kept their voices low and looked my way.

I pulled my legs into me and let my head rest on the tops of my knees, and closed my eyes.

"I see you weren't thirsty." When I lifted my head, Annie was sitting on the couch next to me. "You didn't even open the Coke," she said.

The woman and Officer Jefferson were still down the hallway. Just past them, I saw a tall man hustling toward us.

"Roger!" Annie stood. They held each other, and just before she pulled away, Annie wiped her eyes.

"Why? How?" Annie hugged him again and said, "I'm so glad you're here."

"I wish I'd gotten here sooner. When you called this morning after the funeral, I had a bad feeling. How are you doing kiddo?" Mr. Williamson patted me on the knee.

I shrugged my shoulders.

"I went to the diner first." Mr. Williamson pulled a chair over from the other side of the room as Annie sat beside me again. "I talked to some of the officers there and they told me you'd be here. I see you got fixed up."

"Lacy," Annie said and straightened up. "I need to tell you some things. Tommy just got out of surgery, and it looks good. He's lost a lot of blood, they had to give him a transfusion, but the doctors say he's gonna make it."

"I thought he was dead." Not trusting Annie's words, I asked her, "He's gonna make it? He's gonna live?"

"Well, right now, he's stable. He's in ICU, but the doctors are very hopeful. The bullet missed his organs. He does have a punctured lung, but that was from the bullet breaking a rib."

I couldn't believe it. He was alive. My thoughts went to Samuel Mitchell.

"And what about—"

"Samuel's still in surgery."

"Excuse me." Officer Jefferson approached. "I need to speak with Miss Mitchell, and this is Leslie from Child Protective Services."

"Can this wait? Lacy has been through enough tonight," Annie said.

"Miss ...?" Officer Jefferson held out his hand for Annie to shake it.

"Smith, her last name is Smith." Roger reached across Annie and shook the officer's hand. "And I'm Roger Williamson, retired Durham PD. I know Captain Barger, I spoke with him over at the site. We'll bring Lacy in tomorrow morning first thing, so you can take her statement."

"First thing in the morning," the officer said. He reached into his shirt pocket, pulled out a small spiral-bound pad, and scribbled on the paper. "Leslie, what do you want to do?"

"We have an emergency shelter you could stay in this

evening. Other teenage girls will be there," Leslie said with a soft voice, trying to be delicate.

Annie pulled Mr. Williamson off to the side and whispered in his ear.

"I don't want to go to some stupid shelter." My voice cracked.

"Leslie, Lacy has been through so much. She has been living with me for the last two months, she's comfortable with me and I've been taking care of her," Annie said.

"I understand what you're telling me, Ms. Smith, but my hands—"

"You didn't let me finish," Annie spoke again. "At this time, we can't ask her father about his wishes, but as you know, her mother passed away last week. Before she did, she gave me legal guardianship of Lacy. I have the papers back at the hotel. If you want, you could follow us there."

"Well ..." Leslie hesitated.

"Follow us or take me at my word. I'll bring the paperwork to the police station tomorrow morning."

Satisfied, Leslie and Officer Jefferson headed down the same hallway they'd came in. I was too tired to think about what to do next, but tonight I was not going to a shelter—and for that, I was thankful.

18

W hen Annie called, the hospital said Tommy's condition was worse. He had a fever, which meant there was an infection. The nurse said he was on heavy doses of antibiotics and the next forty-eight hours would be the hardest part. The nurse suggested we come to the hospital directly after leaving the police station because Samuel's condition was critical, and he wasn't expected to make it through the day. As Annie retold the conversation to me, flashes of blood came into my mind—blood on the table, blood on my hand, blood on the shards of glass on the diner floor, and Tommy's shirt covered in blood.

The police station smelled like burnt coffee and men's deodorant, and the cinder block walls looked like they had been painted with mustard, warm mustard because there were drips everywhere. Officer Jefferson and his partner asked questions, and I tried to tell them what I remembered. I answered the best I could, but they had to repeat a lot of the questions because I wasn't listening. I just wanted to go see Tommy. The other police officer seemed to understand that I couldn't remember everything. Some of the memories were clearer than others and sometimes my memories had no meaning at all to the question.

"Lacy ... Lacy?" Officer Jefferson snapped his fingers to get my attention. "Do you remember your hand touching the gun?"

"No, I told you. I just remember seeing Annie come in from the kitchen and then that's it. I don't remember what happened after that, except for being at the hospital."

"So, you don't remember feeling the gun?"

"I think we're done here." Officer Jefferson's partner stood up and pulled Jefferson off to a desk across the room.

"You okay?" Annie asked me.

How many times had I wished for Samuel Mitchell to die? He really might and it didn't feel like I thought it would feel. His face came into my head—at the diner when he was talking about my mother; the night I left when I was yelling at him, nose to nose; the day he killed the yellow jackets. I shook.

"Did I ... did I shoot him?"

"No, God, no. It was an accident," Annie said and put her arms around me.

I nodded.

Officer Jefferson and his partner walked back over to us and his partner spoke, "Captain Barger looked over the guardianship paperwork, Miss Smith. He said Mrs. Mitchell did it right. Normally, this paperwork would supersede our procedure for Lacy. But since the father is still alive, this will change things. You'll have to get him to terminate his parental rights for you to be the legal guardian. Captain says for now and under the circumstances, Lacy can remain with you. I'll take Leslie a copy of the document later this afternoon, and I'm sure she'll be in touch."

I looked at Annie. The words *for now* rang in my ears. What happens if Samuel Mitchell lives? My heart pounded. I would never live with him again, I'd run again. *It won't matter, it won't matter.* I took a breath in. *Soon I'll be with my real father. The truth will come out.*

"Can I see the paper?" I said out loud. Annie asked Officer Jefferson to get the paperwork. He grabbed it off the top of his desk, and as he walked toward me, the paper seemed to float in the air.

In the matter of the child Lacy Marie Mitchell, born August 23, 1965 …. I went to the end of the page. There it was, the line for father's name. It was blank. My mother's signature was under the mother's name line, and Annie's signature, written in big flowing letters, overlapped the printed words around it.

I remember thinking at the time how simple it could have all been if Samuel was dead—a piece of paper and some ink and freedom. And then I wondered how my mother knew I was going to need this legal document. Why hadn't she just written Tommy's name on that line?

She had tried to take care of me, but Samuel Mitchell wouldn't let things be easy.

WHEN WE WENT BACK to the hospital later that day, the doctor told me that the bullet had pierced Samuel's liver and lung and was lodged in a muscle in his back. He went on to explain that there was a good chance for complications. And later that week, the bile from his ripped liver filled his lung which meant another surgery. For eight days, Samuel lingered on the edge of death, the infection taking over his body.

But he didn't die.

Tommy's health improved, the antibiotics worked, and after two weeks, he was moved to a regular room. Right after the shooting, Tommy's wife and son came to be with him. His five-year-old son, Jared, was a miniature Tommy. He talked all the time, asking me questions or telling me random facts. I wanted to not like him, but he had the Franco smile. And I'd never had any siblings, and as brothers went, I supposed Jared was going to be something I could get used to.

Soon after being moved to his own room, Tommy was able to have visitors, and he could actually communicate with them. His wife and Jared came out of the room just as Annie, Roger, and I got there.

"We're going to the cafeteria to get something to eat. He's been asking to see you this morning," Tommy's wife said as she held Jared's hand, walking toward the elevator.

"Hi, Lacy!" Jared smiled over his shoulder at me. "Can I push the button?" he said to his mother.

Annie and Roger said they were going to get coffee. The room was small and had only one bed. He saw me and smiled. Tommy looked so different from my mother; he looked good, alive, and a lot better than the glimpses I'd gotten of him in ICU.

"Hey," he said.

"How are you feeling?"

"Much better. In about a week, they're going to release me to my doctor's care. I'm going home."

"That's good," I said, but didn't mean it. I wondered where that was going to leave me.

"We need to discuss some things."

"Okay." I sat in the blue vinyl chair at the foot of the bed.

"Come closer, just pull that over here," Tommy said, motioning me to the bed. I raised my bottom off the chair and dragged it across the floor, and the wooden legs screeched against the tile.

"You know, you're one lucky girl to have found Annie and Roger."

"Yep, I know."

"I need you to make me a promise. Sometime soon, when

Samuel can have visitors, I want you to go to see him. With Annie and Roger, of course."

"No, I can't do that," I said.

"Please, it's really important to me. What I have to tell you will affect your relationship with him, and I need to know that you will go and see him one more time."

"Why would you want me to see him? You know he's going to jail for what he did to you?"

"I know that, Lacy. But you have to promise me you'll see him before he leaves this hospital."

"I'll go for you."

Tommy closed his eyes. "God, I'm really not good at this kind of thing." He opened them and spoke. "Roger and Annie have been looking into things for us. Roger was able, with his connections, to get a look at the police report, and Annie, being your temporary legal guardian, had access to your medical files." Tommy rested his head on the pillow. "Listen, I want you to know, you are family to me now, no matter what. Do you understand me?" He smiled, but it wasn't the full Franco it's-going-to-be-okay smile.

I nodded.

"Lacy, I know you've been through a lot. I asked Annie and Roger if I could be the one to tell you this." He looked to the ceiling and then into my eyes. "I'm not your father."

What? I thought I'd heard him wrong. "Yes, you *are* my father. Look at us—same hair, and I'm like you. I'm like you in a lot of ways. I know you're my father!" I stood up and leaned down closer to his face. "How can you say that?"

"Wait, now, I want to explain. Sit, please."

I sat.

"At the diner, we all lost blood. The police had to find out the types to put that in their report. Roger looked at the report and asked Annie to find out your mother's blood type. Lacy, I have type B, you have A, your mother was O, and Samuel is A." Tommy looked at me with a sad face and expected me to understand what the letters meant.

"I know this all sounds crazy, but Roger dealt with this kind of thing before he retired. There is no way your mother and I could have made a baby with an A blood type. I can't be your father."

"All this was for nothing." I pushed the chair away from me; it toppled over and I kicked it into the wall. "My running away, looking for you. Nothing!" I yelled and tears came so fast that I couldn't breathe. "My mom's dead because I went searching for nothing!"

"It's not for *nothing*. And you didn't cause your mother's death. I think you know that." His voice was soft and tears rolled down his cheeks. "Come here, please."

At the edge of his bed, I forced myself to stop crying, but my body kept shaking. Tommy touched my face. "Lacy, finding me has been about something. I want you to come and live with me. My wife and I want you to come and be our daughter." And then my dam broke, and I started to cry again. "Of course, the decision is yours," he said.

"You still want me, even if I'm not yours?"

"Yes." Tommy pulled me into him for a one-armed hug. "Lacy, you have so many people who care about you. People you wouldn't have known if you hadn't been searching for me." He pulled me tighter and whispered, "So, really think about it .... Everything that has happened to you has been *something*, not nothing."

~

I did keep my promise to Tommy. The day Annie, Roger, and I left for home, I went to see Samuel. It really wasn't much of a visit, he sat tucked in the hospital bed staring straight ahead and never acknowledged me or anyone else in the room. The nurse came in and took his vitals while we were there. He did everything she asked, so I know he could hear and understand. "He's a real talker," the nurse said and left. After his stay at the hospital, Samuel went to prison with a bullet still lodged in is back.

For two months, I lived with Tommy and his family. They were great to me, but it wasn't right. I missed Annie. It's funny how you want something so much, and when you get it, it turns out that you really needed something different. Something you never would have picked for yourself.

I am lucky to have Annie and Roger in my life. Tommy and his family too—we still keep in touch.

After I left Tommy's house, I wished my life could have been like Jared's. Two great parents, no drinking and hitting. I guess everybody wishes for their life to be different in some way, but now at almost twenty years old, I know Jared's life wasn't mine.

The summer of my fifteenth birthday, I went to see Samuel again. There were lots of things that led to me going to the prison. I didn't want to admit it then, but I wanted him to accept me. Accept the fact that I was his. He had signed away his rights to me and mailed the paperwork to Annie, it was just too easy. And he didn't deserve for things to be that easy. I was his, didn't that make a difference to him? Wasn't that why he treated me the way he did? I wanted answers.

When he came into the visiting room, he was a shell of the person he was before. Annie and I sat, waiting for him at a table. He hovered in the doorway. As I stood and moved in his direction, he turned to the guard and motioned to be taken back inside the prison. A guard approached me and started to escort me out of the visitor's room. I pulled free and yelled across the room, "I am your daughter, I am yours."

I know he heard me. I know it. All that hoping for him not to be my father didn't change the fact that he was. Why didn't he love me?

After my visit, he died two weeks later, to the day. I felt like I'd killed him twice. Still do.

I wonder what would have happened if I hadn't run away that spring. Would they both be here? Would they have magically changed and been the parents I wanted so desperately for them to be? Of course my head says no, but my heart wants to believe things could have been different.

When I first got your letter, I didn't even want to think about you. I imagined that you must hate me so much for what I did. It was an accident. I know that, I'd been told that over and over. And I know that he died in prison not because of me, but from complications from the gunshot wound.

I know I shouldn't, but I blame myself for what happened to Samuel. Roger has told me that it was Samuel's finger on the trigger, not mine. What would have happened if I hadn't rushed him?

Annie would be dead, I always tell myself, and in some weird way, I feel better. I know that's probably not the right thing to say to you. And I'm sorry. But sometimes it's the only thing that helps me understand why everything happened the way it did.

And even though my counselor (Annie wanted me to talk about my feelings to a professional) told me I wasn't responsible for my parents being alcoholics, I can't help but think I was the cause. Maybe if Samuel had really known I was his from the beginning, our lives wouldn't have been filled with such mistrust and hatred. But, he didn't.

In all my letters to you, I have been completely honest. You have brought up things in me that I have pushed down into myself for six years.

Today, I was thinking of my mother's advice, face the truth head-on. If you come, your visit will be finally facing the truth head-on.

So, maybe I'll see you soon.

It's so dry and hot here. No rain. Well, none of any importance. Annie's really worried about the berries.

I'm looking forward to your visit.

Lacy

19

A s Lacy closed up the berry shed for the day, an older black car pulled into the driveway. She knew it was her. Early by a couple of hours, but Lacy knew it was her. The car rolled along the driveway, and Lacy felt like she was in a movie—one of those B movies where at the end a long-lost love meets up with the love of their life, the couple kisses, and everyone lives happily ever after.

They had ended their correspondence completely open to any possibilities, and Lacy wasn't sure how the story had affected her. She had come, Lacy reminded herself. That was a good sign, maybe there would be a happy ending in real life. The car stopped, the engine turned off. The driver, hidden by the setting sun, sat in the car for what seemed to Lacy an eternity.

Before Lacy could reach the front of the car, Annie and Roger were standing on the front porch. Lacy stood and waited. The car door opened, and the tall dark-haired woman stepped out. Lacy was overwhelmed by how much her grandmother looked like Samuel, or how much Samuel had looked like his mother, she corrected her mind. The brown hair—Lacy could tell it was dyed to keep the gray from peeking through, but the color fit her, it was natural—was a match, but the most striking feature was her grandmother's chocolate-brown eyes. The same brown as Samuel and Lacy, exactly.

Lacy kept still and searched the woman's eyes for forgiveness. The woman went to Lacy, cradled her chin with her hand and said, "Let me look at you." She stared at Lacy's face. "God, you look just like him." She pulled Lacy into her arms. Her grandmother squeezed so tight, Lacy could hardly breathe.

Her grandmother pulled back, looked again at Lacy, and wiped mascara-stained tears from her face. Lacy hadn't expected this kind of greeting and stood silent, staring at her grandmother's long flowing skirt and silver anklet with bells. Her grandmother was a gypsy.

Roger and Annie moved toward the car.

"Can I help you get your bags inside?" Roger said.

"My, yes. Now, who is this fine young specimen?" her grandmother asked to no one in particular. Her silver bangle bracelets clinked as she wiped under her eyes again.

"This is Roger, my husband," Annie said with a smile and held her hand out for the woman to shake. "It is so nice to finally meet you, Dorothy."

"Dora, please call me Dora. I changed it long ago for the stage and really don't answer to anything else."

"Your bags?" Roger asked.

"Oh, they're in the back. Has anyone ever told you you look just like Rock Hudson?" Dora said and pitched the keys to Roger.

"Not lately." Roger smiled and looked at Annie.

"We have so much to catch up on, don't we dear." Dora looped her arm around Lacy's waist and started them both toward the front door.

Their dinner conversation was a litany of all the shows that

Dora had performed in. She had been in Shakespeare's *Twelfth Night* twelve times. It was her claim to fame in her theatre community, and she had been Hermia four out of those twelve. Lacy sat mesmerized by her stories and her mannerisms all through the meal. Her father was nothing like his mother.

"Why don't you ladies head on out to the back porch and chat, I'll clean up in here." Roger said.

"Do you have a brother?" Dora lightly touched Roger's shoulder.

HEAT LIGHTNING FLASHED in the distance, lighting up the far corner of the berry field. Annie sat by the door in the wooden rocker, Lacy plopped into the oversize wicker chair, and Dora took over the glider. The wet air settled around them as they sat in silence. Lacy and Dora spoke at the same time.

"You go first," Lacy said.

"I was just going to say, I want to put your mind at ease. I know what happened wasn't your fault." Dora fixed her skirt and spoke again. "You still blame yourself, it's written all over your face, and if you don't let that worry go, when you get to my age, you're going to have deep wrinkles in your forehead."

Annie smiled. Lacy looked out at the sky. It was night but not quite black, it was the purple time. In the distance, a bolt of lightning broke across the sky.

"Look at these wrinkles." Dora pointed to her forehead. "These are deep wrinkles because I didn't forgive myself. I could have never lived the life that Samuel's father wanted. He wanted someone else, but he was in love with the idea of me." Dora twisted her hair over to one side and wiped the sweat from the back of her neck.

"I could never stay in one place for very long. Still can't."

"Did you love him?" Lacy asked.

"Which him?"

"Samuel?"

"I did. I loved him as much as I could love someone. I cared deeply for his father, but I'm in love with life."

"I'm going to get us some lemonade, ladies," Annie said.

"It's too late for my wrinkles dear, but not for yours. I'm here because I want to get to know you. I want a second chance. It's too late with Samuel, but you, well, you don't know me."

"I know that even after everything that happened, you're still here," Lacy said.

"Yeah, I'm here. Four years late."

"What?"

"You asked me in one of your letters how I found you. Remember?"

Lacy nodded.

"Samuel called me from prison a little more than four years ago. I don't know how he found me. Prison connections?" Dora shrugged her shoulders. "It wasn't a long-lost, *Hi, Mom, it's so great to hear your voice* call. No. This was a get-right-to-business call. Now that I think about it, he didn't even say hello. That's how Samuel's father was too; no time for dramatics, for passion." Dora wiped her neck with the hem of her skirt and then fanned herself before letting the material fall. "Anyhow, Samuel said to me I had screwed his life up, and he's right—I'll give him that. He went on to say that if I wanted to make it right between him and I, I needed to get in touch with you and be in your life. 'Treat her right,' were his final words before he hung up."

Lacy stood and tried to understand what this meant. Her gaze scanned the dry berry bushes. She closed her eyes and listened as their leaves rattled in the wind. She opened her eyes and watched a collection of moths flitter around the lamppost at the edge of the field, running her finger across the wood porch railing.

"I know, I know. This is the part I feel terrible about. The four years," Dora said raising her voice to get Lacy's attention.

"He said 'treat her right'?" Lacy said and faced Dora.

Dora nodded and rose from the glider. "I'll be right back, I have something for you," she said and slid into the house.

When Dora returned, she handed Lacy a tattered cigar box. Lacy flipped open the lid, a white owl perched on a cigar surrounded by gold trim sat under the words Blended with Havana. Inside the box, she saw familiar faces. A photo of her mother lay on top; she lifted the picture and then looked at the eyes of the small child in the next photo. After a moment, she realized the child was her. The next photo was her seventh-grade school portrait, and the last photo was Samuel and her mother on their wedding day.

"Those were up on the walls of his cell. In the only way he could, he cared for you," Dora said.

A blue-white bolt of lightning struck the ground in the distance and lit the sky. A few seconds later, a rumble of thunder followed. Lacy flipped through the photos again, and a sense of peace came into her.

"Lacy, I'm not good at staying in one place, or with one person for that matter. When Samuel called, I was right in the middle of a five-week run of *Fiddler on the Roof*. I threw your address in with some costumes and temporarily lost it. But you stayed on my mind the whole time. Costume spring cleaning led me to you. How's that for dramatic?"

Dora patted the glider and Lacy sat beside her.

"I'm not the greatest at taking care of people, I won't be a great grandmother either, but I'll guarantee that your friends won't have grandmothers like me."

Lacy laughed. "I don't need anyone to take care of me, I'm

here with Annie during the summers and at Duke during the school year, but I would like to get to know you better."

Dora stood up and tossed her hair. "I'm Dora Mae Sanders Mitchell, I've been in *Twelfth Night* twelve times, I drive a black Monte Carlo, and my favorite food is biscuits and gravy."

"I'm Lacy Marie Mitchell, a part-time blueberry farmer, a sophomore at Duke studying biology, and the only almost-twenty-year-old I know who has deep wrinkles."

"No, honey, you don't have deep wrinkles yet." Dora opened the screen door for Annie.

Annie held out a wedge of three glasses of lemonade in front of me and I wiggled one free. "Lacy Marie, how did you get that name?" Dora asked.

"I was named after my other grandmother, Marie, and the Lacy came from the wildflower Queen Anne's lace."

"A wildflower, that's beautiful and very dreamy," Dora said, looking up into the night sky.

Annie handed Dora her glass, "Not only is Queen Anne's lace a beautiful wildflower, it's a hardy plant and can grow anywhere."

"Annie, you're so practical and a very lucky woman to be married to Rock Hudson. I'm glad Lacy has you in her life." Dora sipped her lemonade and let out a sigh.

The pitter-patter of raindrops slapped against the dry dirt. Annie moved to the edge of the porch. With a loud clap of thunder, the sky released.

Rain fell.

Annie stepped out into the sheets of water and twirled herself around. She put her face up to the sky and yelled, "Thank God!"

Lacy watched as Annie embraced the rain.

Dora kicked off her shoes and ran to join Annie. They spun around like two little girls at a square dance, spinning themselves so hard. Their wet arms slid apart and they both fell to the ground laughing. Dora called to Lacy, but her words were broken by the force of the rain.

Lacy walked to the end of the porch and stuck her hands past the eves of the roof. Cool droplets of rain dripped from her fingers. With her hands, she made a cup, collected a bowl full of rain and slowly released it, thinking about how this water was what the farm desperately needed.

Before Lacy could pull her hands back out of the rain, Annie and Dora grabbed her hands and pulled her off the porch. In the yard, Dora and Annie danced around Lacy, shouting to her to dance with them. As the rain washed over her body, Lacy raised her chin to the sky, closed her eyes, and soaked in the laughter and joy that surrounded her.

ALSO BY DAWN GARDNER

Eyes of the Peacock

The Cotton Blossom

The Jade Butterfly

Searching For Elvis

ACKNOWLEDGMENTS

There are so many people to thank!

The first one is myself. I DID IT! This is my first novel and it has sat on a *"shelf"* for a very long time waiting to be *"shipped"* into the world. I am proud that I didn't quit, and I am so happy to see this story finally come into your hands. So, thank YOU for reading *Queen Anne's Lace*.

I thank my daughters. I wrote most of this story when they were younger. Funny side note, my writer's space was an all-white, paneled 8x8 storage room in the basement. I set up a desk and a chair and lots of Post-it notes on the walls. I had a sign on the door that read DO NOT DISTURB *unless* 1. Someone is bleeding, 2. You are bleeding. Even now, my daughters lovingly refer to my time spent in the 8x8 room.

I thank my mother and my friend Beth, who both were the earliest readers. They actually read the chapters as I produced them. But you know, when your mother tells you your writing is good—well, it's your mom, what else is she going to say? But I am thankful for her constant support and encouragement. Also during this same time period, my fellow writers in my local writer's group were amazing. They helped me fine-tune the story, and I grew as a writer because of their feedback.

Next, my friends Katie and Jim. Honestly, I don't think this novel would have ever seen the light of day without their encouragement! As I watched Jim publish his historical fiction novel, I was so inspired. I thank both of you from the bottom of my heart!

Mike. His name deserves to be a sentence. He always believes in me, always offers me his thoughts and encouragement. We found each other later in life and for that I am truly thankful. I am so happy to be going through this life with him. Thank you, Mike, for all your love and support!

AND now ... I am off to finish my second novel. I can't wait to see where this publishing journey takes me and to share my stories with you!

ABOUT THE AUTHOR

Dawn is an author and a professional photographer. *Queen Anne's Lace* is her first novel. Writing has always been a part of her life in some shape or form. Currently, she is working on two novels for the new year.

Dawn lives in Virginia with her husband and two dogs. She loves being surrounded by family and friends, traveling, reading and outdoor adventures.

dawngardnerauthor.com

instagram.com/dawngardnerauthor

facebook.com/dawngardnerauthor

Made in the USA
Middletown, DE
16 November 2021